Seven Stories Up

ALSO BY LAUREL SNYDER

Bigger than a Bread Box

Penny Dreadful

Any Which Wall

Up and Down the Scratchy Mountains

Seven Stories Up

Laurel Snyder

RANDOM HOUSE NEW YORK

Visit us on the Web! randomhouse.com/kids

Educators and librarians, for a variety of teaching tools,
visit us at RHTeachersLibrarians.com

Library of Congress Cataloging-in-Publication Data
Snyder, Laurel.
Seven stories up / Laurel Snyder. — First edition.
pages cm.
Summary: In 1987, while her mother sits in a Baltimore hotel at the deathbed of a grandmother twelve-year-old Annie never knew, Annie travels back fifty years and shares adventures with the lonely girl who will grow up to be her feisty grandmother.
ISBN 978-0-375-86917-4 (trade) — ISBN 978-0-375-96917-1 (lib.bdg.) —
ISBN 978-0-375-89999-7 (ebook)
[1. Space and time—Fiction. 2. Grandmothers—Fiction. 3. Mothers and daughters—Fiction. 4. Hotels, motels, etc.—Fiction. 5. Baltimore (Md.)—History—20th century—Fiction.] I. Title.
PZ7.N43777Sev 2014 [Fic]—dc23 2013005020

Printed in the United States of America

10 9 8 7 6 5 4 3 2 1

First Edition

Random House Children's Books supports
the First Amendment and celebrates the right to read.

CONTENTS

EACH FRIEND REPRESENTS A WORLD IN US, a world possibly not born until they arrive, and it is only by this meeting that a new world is born.

—ANAÏS NIN

Seven Stories Up

• 1 •

YOU'RE SUPPOSED TO CRY

You're supposed to cry when your grandma is dying. You're supposed to be really sad. But as Mom and I sped through the dark streets of Baltimore, I couldn't stop bouncing in my seat. At last I stuck my head out the window and leaned into the muggy night. My hair whipped around. The sharp rush of air felt good on my face.

I'd always wondered about my grandmother. That might sound funny, but Mom didn't talk about her family at all. If I asked a question, even for a school project, she'd find a way to change the topic. She'd suddenly decide that she had to pay the bills "pronto," or she'd remember that *Dallas* was on TV "right this very minute."

If I kept pushing, she'd make her sad face and say something like, "Kiddo, let's leave that story in the past, where it can't cause trouble." I never understood what exactly the trouble might be, but I didn't like to see Mom unhappy, so I'd learned to invent my own stories. Like in the first grade, when I told Mrs. Johnson that my mom was an orphan princess from Idaho. She'd made me build a diorama about it, in a shoe box. That was how I learned that Idaho is a mountainous region bordering Canada, full of colorful gems and potatoes.

Idaho aside, here's what I knew:

1. My mom grew up in Baltimore but left for college in Atlanta.
2. Her dad had been dead a long time, but her mother was still alive.
3. She had aunts somewhere, who sent big glittery Christmas cards each year.

I also knew that my dad had skipped out on us in 1975, right after I was born, but that was different. Mom didn't mind talking about *him*. She said she couldn't be too mad, even though he was kind of a louse, because without him she wouldn't have me, and I was her very best thing in the world.

We did have one lonely Polaroid of my grandmother in our scrapbook. I was a chubby baby in the picture, and my grandmother, in gray curls and an ugly plaid pantsuit, held me out stiffly to the camera with both hands. She looked afraid she might drop me.

I'd stared at that photo for hours, memorizing her clothes and posture, the paisley wallpaper in the background. I knew her name was Mary. That was all I'd ever expected to know.

Until now! Now I was in a strange city at midnight, racing toward her deathbed. Her *deathbed*? It was like a scene from a movie. If only I could stop imagining her gasping her last breath in a pantsuit.

I pulled my head in the window again and tried to comb my wind-snarled hair with my fingers. Mom had turned the radio on and Michael Jackson was singing softly. I watched the city rush by, row houses lining each street. Everything narrow and brick. As we went over a bridge, I saw boats rocking gently in a harbor. I sneezed at a strong scent of—was it *cinnamon*? Weird.

Without realizing it, I'd started to chew my thumbnail. I could feel the ragged needle of a hangnail with my tongue. I yanked it off with my front teeth, winced, and jammed my hand in the pocket of my jean shorts.

At last Mom turned onto a shadowy tree-lined street and slowed the car to a crawl, inching past enormous town houses with tall doors and tiny squares of garden. After a few blocks, we pulled into a driveway. I unsnapped my seat belt and scrambled out into a wide drive of gray bricks. Staring up at a tall stone building, I forgot to breathe.

It was past midnight, but the moon was full and there were street lamps, so I could make out the grinning gargoyles over the double glass doors. HOTEL CALVERT, read the brass sign that peeked out through a tangle of ivy. I was surprised. Usually we stayed at a Holiday Inn or a HoJo. Someplace cheap, with scratchy sheets and a half-empty candy machine in the lobby.

Mom was rooting in the trunk for our suitcase. I listened to her thump and cuss; then I looked back up at the hotel. That was when I noticed the dark windows. There was just one square of brightness along the side of the building, all the way up on the top floor. One window that blazed. Everything else was dark.

"Hey, Mom," I said slowly. "I don't think this place looks open."

"It *isn't*," Mom said, slamming the trunk. "I have a key."

"You have a *key*?"

Mom started up the overgrown drive with our bag, her clogs clacking in the darkness. I shut my door and hurried after her, stumbling over a loose brick. "Wait," I called. "You said we were going straight to my grandma's house."

"This is it," said Mom, stopping and gesturing tiredly at the hotel.

"This?"

"It's hers."

"The whole thing?"

Mom nodded. "The whole thing. Though I guess it's about to be mine. Or—ours. I grew up here."

"Here?" I stared up at the leering gargoyles. "You grew up *here*?"

She shrugged. "I tried to, anyway."

"Are you kidding me?" I shouted. "This place is amazing, like out of a novel or *Europe* or something!"

Mom sighed as she rooted in her big straw purse. "A novel . . . You don't know the half of it."

"No," I said. "I don't. But this is an even better story than Idaho!"

"Maybe a good *story*," she said grimly. Then she added in a softer tone, "Look, Annie, I know I owe you a lot of explanations. Just—not tonight. Okay?"

"Okay," I said. "But *wow*. You grew up like Eloise."

"Not *quite* like Eloise," said Mom. "I never had a pet turtle." She groaned as she hefted the suitcase up the three moss-covered steps that led to the double doors, but the bag tipped over as rain began to spit down. I caught the bag as it fell. It almost sent me tumbling.

"Rain?" Mom looked up at the sky like she was asking it a question. "Perfect." She grabbed the handle of the suitcase back from me. Then she stuck a key in the lock, opened one of the massive doors, and hurried inside. She called over her shoulder, "Let's get this over with. Then maybe we can watch a movie, if Mother ever figured out how to hook up the VCR I sent."

A movie was the furthest thing from my mind. I stood in the rain and felt the drops hit my face. I stared up at the ledges of the old windows, at curling vines that gripped the stone, at the building above me, which looked like something from a dream.

Then I stepped into the lobby, and it was beyond anything I could have invented or wished for. I let the door fall shut and stared up, up into the tallest room ever. A chandelier hung from the ceiling, an icy shower of diamonds in the darkness. It wasn't on, but it shimmered like magic in the dim light. I felt a tremble, like I was shimmering too.

Mom had already crossed the black-and-white checkerboard floor. Now she turned back to me, at the foot of a marble staircase. "I can't imagine how it must seem to you." She gestured at a grand piano in the corner. "All this glitz. Kinda crazy, huh?"

"Kinda," I said. "But *good* crazy. Totally awesome crazy."

Mom frowned slightly. "I wish I could see it like you're seeing it. For the first time. I guess it *is* totally awesome." Then she added, "Come on," and turned back around to flip a switch that shed warm light down a hallway. "Time's up, kiddo. Let's get gone."

As I followed her across the cavernous room, I sneezed. Dust and cobwebs hung on to every surface: the antique end tables and lamps, the reception desk with its tarnished brass top.

I reached out to touch a statue, a white angel that tiptoed above a pedestal at the foot of the staircase. Beneath the dust, the marble gleamed a bright white. I stared into the angel's face. How many years had she been waiting like that, dusty in the darkness? Alone.

Mom was tapping her foot. "Annie, seriously, come *on*!"

I sprinted over to where she stood in front of an old elevator. The doors were heavy and gilded, engraved with a pattern of vines and flowers. I reached out a hand to feel the grooves in the metal as they slid open.

Inside, Mom pushed the 7 button, the highest number on the panel, and though the button didn't light up, the doors slid together and the elevator began to move. A bell rang when we arrived with a clattering metallic *brrrrring!*

We stepped out into an unlit hallway with wall-to-wall carpet that made it hard to pull the suitcase. I reached up to put a hand on Mom's arm so that I wouldn't trip and fall, as together we fumbled along in the whispery darkness. Farther down we made a right turn, then almost immediately Mom had her keys jangling at another door.

"Great," she grumbled, "now the key is sticking. C'mon. Work!" She kicked at the door.

"Here," I said, "let me try. . . ."

I leaned toward Mom, pushed her hand aside, and turned the key. When I gripped the glass knob, it felt good, smooth and cool in my hand. The door unlocked right away with an even click. I pushed and it swung inward.

"Thanks," said Mom.

We stepped together into a living room that was small and impossibly neat. It was air-conditioned, and the change in temperature took my breath away. I looked around. There was a beige-and-white-striped sofa with a matching recliner. Dried flowers stood in a white vase on a glass coffee table. There were no smudges on the glass. The carpet was creamy and the walls were tan. The room felt bland and unused, like a display in a department store.

Across from us a woman slept upright in a chair with a paperback on her lap. She was wearing green hospital scrubs and purple eye shadow. Beside her chair was a closed door.

"Hello?" Mom called softly.

The lady started and opened her eyes. Without missing a beat, she put a finger to her lips, set her book on the floor, and stood up.

Mom walked across the room and whispered something in the woman's ear. Then they both turned to look at me. The lady shook her tightly permed hair and frowned. I squinted to read her name tag: EMERY ROTH, RN.

"Annie," whispered my mom gently. "You go on ahead in there." She pointed to an open door on the other side of the couch. "Take our stuff and get yourself settled. There's a bathroom, and you can watch TV. Just try not to make too much noise."

"Where are *you* going?" I asked.

She nodded at the closed door beside her. "In here for a sec."

"But I want to go with you," I said.

"No, *ma'am*. What's in that room is not . . . fun."

"I know," I said. "I don't care."

"*You* don't care because you don't get it," Mom said. "This is serious, Annie. It isn't some adventure from a book. My mother is sick, and I need to see her. In case she . . ." She didn't finish her sentence.

"Dies?" I asked.

Mom flinched.

"This might be my only chance," I argued. "I'm old enough to handle it, I promise. I'll be in middle school this fall."

Mom crossed her arms and stared down at me. "Even so, kiddo, you need to trust me on this one."

"I'm not scared."

"You're *never* scared," said Mom. She leaned down and touched my face. "But this isn't about you, Annie. Please? Help me out here?"

I could have argued with her, but Mom looked so tense I actually *did* feel a little scared. "O-okay," I said.

Mom straightened up, turned her back on me, twisted the knob, and slipped through the door. Emery Roth, RN, sat back down and picked up her book as if I wasn't there, so I dragged our suitcase away, carving a groove in the plush carpet.

There wasn't much to look at in the other room. Just furniture, a small television, and an open door that led to a bathroom. I looked out the one window and saw that it was raining harder. In the distance, lightning flashed above the clouds, but I didn't hear thunder. I guessed it was still too far away.

Along one wall there was a display of framed photos. The pictures were mostly black-and-white, but a few were in color. I leaned in for a better look.

The color photos were of a young couple and their curly-haired baby. Was that Mom? I guessed so. The dad wore a hat and had a thin mustache. The mom was delicate and pretty, with dark curls and red lips. I could see how she might grow into a gray-haired grandma in a pantsuit. The man and woman weren't touching. Not one arm around a shoulder. No smiles.

The older photos, the black-and-white ones, were of a larger family, all dressed up in old-timey clothes, derby hats and frilly dresses. Most of those shots were of special occasions, Christmases and weddings, taken in the lobby downstairs. Were these the glittery Christmas card aunts? Maggie? Ginny?

On a low shelf in the cabinet beneath the bedside table, I came across a scrapbook, with fancy gold lettering that read MY SCHOOL DAYS. I flipped it open, and the delicate paper tore away from the binding. *Property of Mary Moran*, the torn page read in cramped, careful handwriting. I began to turn the pages gently, but the book was almost empty. There were a few birthday cards, and clippings from newspapers: about Amelia Earhart, John F. Kennedy, Princess Elizabeth. I found a curl of dark hair tied with a tiny ribbon, and a couple of dead earwigs. That was it. No love letters. No secrets.

I put the scrapbook back and heaved our suitcase onto the flowered bedspread so I could pull out my nightgown and kit bag. Then I walked into the bathroom to arrange my stuff: toothbrush, inhaler, vitamins, hairbrush, and my prized strawberry Lip Smacker, the only makeup Mom allowed.

That was when I heard voices. Sharp but quiet sounds, murmurs coming from the towel rack mounted on the back of a white door. I knew I shouldn't do it, but I couldn't stop myself. I reached behind the soft folds of terry cloth and felt for a knob. When I turned it, I crossed my fingers. The door opened a crack, and a sharp smell wafted in at me, a mixture of carnations and poison. A hospital smell.

On the other side of the door, in a dimly lit room, my mom stood beside a bed. I put my ear to the crack and strained to make out the voices. It wasn't easy, because of another sound, a machine that wheezed and hissed like a gasping metronome. I listened hard.

"No, Mother—calm down," Mom was saying. "It's not like that."

"Isn't it, Ruby?" said a shaky voice. Then I heard a shallow rattle of coughs.

I closed my eyes and swallowed hard as I had a sudden flash of memory. My best friend Susie had a Grandma Roxy, a loud woman who shouted "Hells bells!" and wore hot-pink lipstick. Grandma Roxy had once taken me along for a fancy lunch and a manicure with Susie. I'd loved that day! The three of us laughing, joking, toasting with our Shirley Temples (me and Susie) and pink wine (Roxy). Secretly I'd pretended Susie and I were cousins, that Roxy was my grandma too.

For some reason, when I heard the voice through the bathroom door, that thin wheeze, I thought of Roxy. There was nothing loud and laughing about my real grandmother.

For a minute I listened to the machine gasping. I wondered if the old woman had fallen asleep. Or maybe it was over already. Could people die that fast? I opened the door a little further. Mom was sitting beside the bed.

Then I heard the tired voice rasp out, "Hello! Hello? Who's there?"

I froze.

I waited.

Nothing happened for a second. But when I tried to close the door, it creaked, and the raspy voice called again. "Who is it? I know you're here. Come out where I can see you!"

Definitely not dead.

• 2 •

LIKE A SMALL SHARP KNIFE

"Annie!" Mom was glaring at me.

"Sorry," I mouthed at her.

"Annie? Is that you?" gasped the old lady. "Are *you* here?"

"Yeah. It's m-me," I stuttered as I swung the door all the way open and stepped in. My voice felt faint, caught in my throat. Like it belonged to a shy kid in a school play. Not my voice at all.

I could see now that the old woman in the bed was connected to machines and propped against large white pillows. Her skin was so pale I could make out her veins, and her wispy gray hair reminded me of a dandelion clock, ready to blow away. She was staring at me, her eyes big in her narrow face.

"You don't look . . . like your pictures," she said, squinting. She had to stop for a breath in the middle of her sentence. "Your hair . . . is longer."

"It is?" I touched my hair.

"It's been a year since the last batch of pictures, Mother," said Mom softly. "I've been busy, and she grows so fast. It's hard to keep up."

That was when I realized that while Mom hadn't told me anything at all about my grandmother, she had been writing home to Baltimore about me. Sending updates, like people did in normal families.

"Come . . . closer," my grandmother called. "Let me . . . look at you." A frail hand stirred the air above the bed.

I forced my feet forward. "Hi," I said, trying to sound like myself. I cleared my throat. "Hi!"

My grandmother raised her head from the pillow a few inches and peered up at me. "She's . . . pretty," she said to Mom.

"Yes," said my mom. "She looks a lot like you."

Staring at the withered face against the pillows, I didn't want that to be true, but I could see what Mom meant. My grandmother's high forehead was my own.

Her dark brown eyes. Her pointy chin. I leaned forward until my arms were touching the metal rail of the hospital bed.

My grandmother propped herself up a little. "Annie, I'm glad . . . to see you."

"Umm, yeah, me too," I said.

"Is that true?" she asked in a sharper voice. "*Are* you glad to see me?"

"Umm, yeah," I mumbled.

The old woman stared a little too long. I felt funny. At last she took a deep, harsh breath from her oxygen mask, then said, "So . . . you must know I'm dying?"

"Now, Mother," said Mom, standing up beside me. "Anything could happen. You might feel better tomorrow."

The old woman scowled. To me, she said, "She has a bad habit . . . of always looking . . . at the bright side. Have you noticed?"

"I—I guess," I said.

Beside me, Mom muttered something I couldn't make out.

The old woman leaned toward me. "Annie," she said, "I realize we don't . . . know each other well, but . . . there isn't much time. And I want you to know you're . . . important to me. I think about you, dear."

"Uh, okay. Thanks," I said.

She paused, then added, "And I *do* hope . . . I'm . . . important to you?"

"Huh?" At first I thought she must be talking to Mom, but she was staring straight at me. I shifted my weight from one foot to the other. "Sure, yeah," I said at last. "I mean, *yes*."

"Yes?" She raised her eyebrows. "You *do* care for me?"

I nodded dumbly.

"You . . . *love* me?" She sucked at the oxygen mask again, waiting.

"I . . . uh . . ." I glanced at Mom. She covered her mouth with her hand and shook her head slightly.

Why would she ask that? How *could* I love her? I'd never even seen her until this minute. I stared at my grandmother's whiskers, just a few silver hairs on her chin. I was close enough to count them. Six. There were six.

"Well, *do* you?" she rasped again. "Love me?"

"I—don't—know," I said, glancing from my mom to my grandmother. "I mean—sure."

Her eyes narrowed. "*Sure?* You don't sound very certain."

"Mother!" Mom cut her off. "Stop. You're a stranger to her."

I stepped back from the bed as my grandmother turned

to Mom. She spat out her next words. "Well, whose fault is *that*, Ruby?"

Panic flitted across Mom's face. I'd never seen her like that, ever. She looked like a scared kid. Suddenly I caught a glimmer of what she'd run away from. My grandmother wasn't just old and sick. She was *angry*.

"Leave Mom alone," I whispered.

My grandmother didn't relent. "How about *you*, Ruby? Do *you* love me?"

Mom looked ready to cry. I wished I'd stayed in the other room.

"Of course I do," Mom said softly. "But sometimes—love isn't enough."

"No, I suppose it isn't," said my grandmother, falling back against her pillows. "I guess it never was with you."

Mom waited. The room felt electric, charged. At last she said in a small voice, "I was only a little girl. . . ."

"A heartless girl, always running off." My grandmother frowned at the ceiling.

"Mother—please don't," Mom said with tears in her eyes.

"Don't what?" My grandmother fixed her gaze on Mom. "What is it you want me *not* to do, Ruby?" She cocked her chin sharply to one side and raised her arched eyebrows. It was a strained gesture, awkward. "What *can* I do? Locked in the Lonely Room. Just like all those years ago. Nothing ever changes, not for me."

It was awful, but I couldn't turn my eyes away. It was like a bloody nature show you can't stop watching, where a shark eats a seal or a lion takes down an antelope.

Mom ran a hand through her hair limply. "You know what, Mother? It's after midnight. Annie doesn't need to be here for this. In the morning we can talk. Things will be better—"

"Oh? You think so?"

Mom looked sadly at the old woman; then she turned and pushed me toward the door. "Scoot," she said gently.

I started to scoot.

"Fine, run away," wheezed my grandmother. "But if you do, I will die. Tonight. It's one thing I *can* still do."

Then it was like a spell had broken. I turned to watch as Mom pivoted slowly on one foot, to face the old woman in the bed. She put her hands on her hips and pulled herself up tall. "All right, *fine*," she said. "Die if you want! I came here to be with you, Mother, but for twelve years I've kept Annie safe, and I'm not undoing that. I'll be back in the morning, because I want to see you. *Not* because you're playing head games with me. Got it?"

"Oh? You want to *see* me?" my grandmother called.

"You've been gone all these years, but now you want to see me die, Ruby? *This* you came for?"

Mom paused a moment, then said, "Of course I came, Mother. Because no matter what you choose to think—I *do* love you."

Without opening her eyes or raising her head, my grandmother spoke. Her voice was clear, and there was a slight curve to her mouth, a smile like a small sharp knife. "Yes, well," she said, "*you* love a lot of people."

Mom jerked the bathroom door hard behind her, then stood for a second with her face in one hand. "So," she said, "you wanted to meet your grandmother. Good times, huh?"

"Yeah," I said. "I'm sorry."

Mom splashed some water on her face, then rubbed it dry with a towel. When she was done, I padded after her into the bedroom, where we sat on the edge of the bed. Mom stared at the pictures on the wall.

"It used to be a beautiful hotel," she said. "It used to be a beautiful family. Once upon a time . . ."

"Hey," I said. "Mom?"

"What is it, kiddo?" Her voice was tender.

"I understand now why you kept her so secret. I get it. But if you'd explained, I bet I could have handled it."

Mom spread out her fingers in a helpless gesture. "Maybe *I* couldn't handle it. Or maybe I just didn't know where to begin, or when. You were too little, until one day you weren't anymore, but it was still such a hard story. I've never known how to tell it."

"Well, *now* can you tell me—what's wrong with her?"

Mom shook her head. "I wish I knew. She's just always been like that. Angry. Or maybe *angry* isn't the right word. I'm not sure what is. Desperate? When I was a kid, whatever I did—it wasn't enough. Nothing was ever enough. I'd come home nervous and take a deep breath at the door before I walked in. I was *always* nervous. Kids shouldn't grow up that way."

"No."

"The thing is, it wasn't just me. To hear her tell it, I abandoned her. But so did everyone else. Her parents neglected her. Dad didn't listen. Her sisters were mean. Every waiter in every restaurant has been disrespectful. It's like she's got a big black hole inside. Like she's hungry and can't get full, no matter how people try to feed her. Ugh."

"Wasn't there anyone who could help?" I asked. "A doctor, maybe?"

"You're a good kid, Annie. I felt that way too. I tried to help for a long time. But it's only gotten worse over the years. When my dad died and I moved to Atlanta, something snapped inside her. That was when she closed the hotel up, told me never to bother coming home. I was eighteen years old."

"*Really?* What did you do?" I asked.

"I stayed gone, started over. I got an apartment near campus, married your father, made the best of it. Honestly, I felt guilty but relieved."

"It sounds hard."

"It was easier. I got to choose my friends, make my own family. You get it?"

"I think so."

Mom stood up. "Look, you go ahead and crash. I need to take a walk, clear my head. I'll feel better in the morning, I promise."

"But it's raining," I said, looking out the window.

Mom laughed. "I'll be fine. A walk in the rain never hurt anyone."

When she was gone, I pushed the suitcase as hard as I could. It fell off the bed with a crash, but it didn't matter. The floors below were empty. There was nobody to hear.

It was past late, so I got ready for bed. I settled into

the pillows, pulled the covers up, and burrowed down. But when I turned over to shut off the light beside me, something hard jabbed me in the neck. I sat up, slipped a hand beneath the pillow, and brought out a book, folded in heavy black cloth.

It was an old copy of *The Secret Garden*. Inside was an inscription: *To Mary Moran, from her mother.* I ran my hand over the worn cover. I wondered how long it had been forgotten in those pillows. I wondered why an old lady would be reading it, anyway.

I set the book beside me on the bedside table and began to lay the black cloth on top of it, when I realized that what I was holding was a sleeping mask. It was made of silk, stitched with tiny black beads.

Like the book, the mask was falling apart. The elastic had lost its stretch. The silk was faded and heavy, the beads coming loose. I pulled it on like a headband. It felt nice, smooth against my forehead.

I lay back, my head on the thick pillow, listening to rain pelting the window. Off in the distance there was a loud rumble of thunder. The storm was getting closer, and Mom was out there in it, alone and sad. I stared up at the faded canopy with its rips and stains, and wished there was a way to fix everything for her.

At last I began to pull the heavy silk over my eyes.

Just as I slipped the mask all the way down, there was a strange moment of static in the air, a beat of absolute silence . . . then another huge burst of thunder.

I flinched.

And the world went dark.

· 3 ·

WHO DOESN'T LIKE MUFFINS?

"Hello? Hello!"

Deep inside my dream there was a voice. I wanted to answer it, but everything was dark, muffled. My head was thick. My body wouldn't wake up. My mouth wouldn't move.

Until I heard the voice again. "Hellllloooo?"

I started to surface.

"Who *are* you?" The voice broke through. It was a girl's voice. I could feel her breath on my face. "And what on earth are you doing here?"

Something touched my cheek. "Huh!" I sat up fast and opened my eyes.

Everything was still dark. I couldn't see. Why couldn't I see?

Then I remembered, reached up, and yanked the mask off. My eyes were flooded with thin, early-morning light.

"I have a sleeping mask like that too," said the voice. "Only I never wear it."

I whipped around, and there she was. A kid. Staring at me. A girl in a long ivory nightgown, with eyes as dark as mine, nearly hidden beneath a mop of brown curls. A girl, sitting in my bed!

"But how did you get in here?" she asked.

She was too close. It was weird. Her knee brushed my bare arm and I jerked back, lost my balance, and rolled from the high mattress onto the floor. Ouch. Just like my suitcase had done the night before. Though, now that I looked, I didn't see the suitcase. From my tangle of sheets and blankets I could only spot the black sleeping mask, which had fallen with me. I sat up and rubbed my bruised knee.

The girl was peering over the edge of the mattress. Her ringlets clustered and hung, framing her narrow face. "I *am* sorry," she said. She shook her head, and her curls trembled. "I didn't mean to scare you."

"O-okay," I said. "I guess. But what'd you do with my suitcase?"

The girl looked puzzled. She tilted her head. "What suitcase?"

"The one that was right *here*!" I thumped the floor beside me.

"I didn't see a suitcase," she said. "Why would you bring a suitcase?"

"I'm—I just—" I looked around, baffled. "I went to sleep. That's all I did." Maybe I was *still* asleep and dreaming. Was that possible? Everything from the day before felt hazy. "I *think* I went to sleep here." That had to be right. I recognized the big bed, its high canopy. "How did *you* get in?"

"This is my room, silly," said the girl, sitting back on her feet. "I'm always here." Her brow creased. "Maybe the door was open, and you sleepwalked?"

Her room? From my spot on the floor, I tried to figure out what was going on. The bed looked the same, but maybe the girl was right—maybe this *wasn't* the room I'd fallen asleep in. Maybe all the rooms in the hotel had beds like that. Now that I thought about it, the striped bedspread did seem different.

But propped beside the lamp on the bedside table was a black-and-white picture I thought I'd seen before. Or

I'd seen something like it anyway. A photo of a couple, dressed in old-fashioned clothes. I had a flash of memory. I whirled around to look for the other pictures on the wall behind me. There was only a large painting of a small fat dog sitting on a small fat pillow.

This wasn't the same room! *Had* I sleepwalked? Either way, what was this girl doing in the deserted hotel?

"I'm sorry," I said. "I didn't mean to freak you out. I thought this was the room I went to sleep in."

"*Freak* me out." The girl repeated my words slowly. She burst out laughing. "I don't know what those words mean, but you're funny. You should stay for breakfast."

"Thanks," I said. "I guess."

As I stood up, I noticed that the canopy on this bed was a pure, fresh white. A breeze from the open window beside me ruffled the crisp curtains. I could hear bird sounds from beyond. The rain was gone.

"You really should," said the girl. "Nora will be here shortly with my tray, and Cook bakes delicious muffins. Will you join me?" She paused for my answer.

Nora? Who was Nora? And Cook? Everything was making less sense by the minute. This couldn't be a deserted hotel if someone was going to be stopping by with room service. I stared out the window at an unfamiliar skyline.

Was it possible that this was some kind of . . . *magic*? An alternate universe? A *Star Trek* wormhole? Had I made a wish without realizing it? I remembered the shimmer when I first set foot in the hotel. I remembered the thunder, the static in the air before I fell asleep. If magic existed anywhere, it probably belonged in a place like this. But *still* . . .

When I didn't respond right away, the girl turned from me sharply. "Never mind," she said. "You don't have to stay for breakfast if you don't want to. I don't care. I'll eat the muffins myself."

"Wait, what?" I said. "Hold the phone! I'm hardly awake over here. Of course I want muffins. Who doesn't like muffins?"

Then the girl's face lit up again. It was like watching a campfire catch. Her smile was quick. Her eyes sparkled. I'd never met anyone who changed moods so quickly.

"Oh, *good*," she said, bouncing on her knees on the bed. "That's settled! Though you might want to put on something more . . . suitable." She waved a hand at my bare legs. "For Nora's sake." The girl reached over, picked up something blue, and tossed it at me. "Here. Try this on."

I slipped the blue robe over my nightgown; it was

smooth, made of rich folds of silk. It reminded me of the sleeping mask. "You can wear it back to your room, then just leave it at the front desk. Tell Mr. McGhee it's for Molly."

"Mr. McGhee?"

"The hotel manager," she said.

"Oh, umm, sure," I said. I guessed this meant I *was* still in the hotel. Only now the hotel wasn't deserted? How could that be?

Then an idea began to form in my mind, a crazy, scary, spectacular idea. "Molly?" I said. "*That's* your name? Molly."

"Yes." The girl put a hand to her chest in a funny formal gesture. "*I'm* Molly."

I stood there, nodding slowly. All the while my brain was scrambling, trying to fit the pieces together. The thought flitting around in my head was so impossible, I couldn't believe I was even having it. But nothing else made sense.

I looked at the photo on the bedside table. The two people in the picture stood in front of a big black car. The man wore a suit and a dark hat pulled low over his forehead. He had a mustache. The woman was staring off into the distance. She was beautiful, in a pale dress and a tiny veiled hat.

Behind me, Molly said, "That's my mother. She's away. But perhaps you saw Papa downstairs?"

I turned back around. "Perhaps," I said slowly. "*Perhaps.*" I tested the word out, and it felt funny in my mouth. *Perhaps* wasn't a word I usually used.

"Which floor are you staying on?" Molly asked. "I don't think you said."

"I—oh, I don't know. That is, I'm not sure I remember." I glanced across the room at a magazine on the dresser. If only I could hold it for a second, I might be able to confirm my impossible suspicion. "Hey," I said, "can you—maybe remind me of today's date? It's, like, the eighteenth, right? August eighteenth?"

Molly shook her head. "It isn't *like* the eighteenth. It *is* the eighteenth."

"Oh, yeah, that's what I meant," I said. "August eighteenth, nineteen . . ."

"Well, 1937, naturally!"

I sat back down on the bed. Hard.

1937?

1937!

Had fifty years just melted away? It wasn't possible. And yet . . .

Molly kept right on chattering. "I don't suppose you

know how to play any card games? I like to play cards during breakfast, when I have company."

"Yeah," I said distractedly. "Sure I do."

Molly beamed. "How nice!"

All the while I was thinking: *Magic? Magic?* It was happening. To me, Annie Jaffin. I'd fallen into a dream, a story, the past. Mom hadn't told me anything about this place, but now I'd get a chance to explore it myself. 1937! What would *that* be like? Flappers? Were flappers from the thirties? Or Marilyn Monroe?

I looked up. Molly was watching me intently, the way she might have watched a TV show (not that she'd ever seen one—I was pretty sure they didn't have TVs in 1937). "You look," she said, "as though you're thinking about something fun."

"You could say that," I said, grinning uncontrollably.

"What is it? Will you tell me?"

"Oh, I can't," I said. "But it's nothing. Really. I promise."

"Please?"

I shook my head. "If I told you," I said, "you'd think I was bonkers."

"Bonkers?"

"Nuts," I said.

She still looked puzzled. "Nuts?"

"Crazy," I said. "Because it's impossible. The thing I'm thinking about."

"Well, I like impossible things," said Molly. "The impossibler, the better."

I wasn't sure what to do. In so many books I'd read, magic was supposed to be a secret. I didn't want to break the rules and have my adventure end before it began. But what if Molly was supposed to be part of my adventure? Maybe Molly and I had a treasure to find or a mystery to unravel. Maybe we were supposed to bring two star-crossed lovers together.

"Okay," I said at last. "Okay, but you have to promise to believe me."

"Oh, I will," she said. She leaned forward, waiting. "My eldest sister says I'll believe *anything*!"

"And you can't laugh!"

"Of *course* not," she said.

I took a deep breath. "See, the truth is—well, I think I just time-traveled."

I sat back and waited for her to register shock, but Molly only looked confused. "I don't understand," she said. "What does that mean? *Time-traveled?*"

"I mean, I think I came here by magic. I don't know how or why, but I'm here from—*the future*."

Molly stared for a minute. She mouthed the words

the future silently. Then suddenly she clapped her hands loudly and shouted, "I did it!"

"You did?"

Molly nodded. "*I* did this. Or I think I did. I wished you here!"

"You *what*?"

"I've been wishing, you see. On stars. Each night, before bed."

"For *me*?"

"For *someone*. Anyone. Now here you are, and you're someone! So it must have worked, my wishing. How else did you get here?"

"I—I don't know," I admitted. It hadn't occurred to me that my adventure might be the result of some random stranger's wish. "I only know that I belong somewhere else. Or some*when*."

"Some*when*? Is that a future word?"

"Oh," I said. "No. In fact, I think maybe I just made it up this minute."

Molly beamed. "Well, in any case, this is marvelous! Until you go back to *somewhen else*, you can stay with me. We'll play and talk. You'll be my secret."

"*Stay* with you?"

Molly nodded vigorously. "You will, won't you? Please? Say yes!"

I shrugged. "Sure. Until the magic sends me home."

"Oh, thank you," Molly said very seriously. "I'm so grateful. You can't begin to imagine." She tilted her head slightly, in a funny practiced way, and when she did, a memory shook loose in my mind. Her dark eyes and the angle of her jaw gave me a flash of déjà vu, a faint memory of a head turned just so.

"You know," said Molly, "you haven't told me *your* name yet."

"Oh!" I said. "I'm Annie. Annie Jaffin."

"Annie. That's pretty," said Molly. "Nice to meet you, Annie Jaffin. I'm Mary Moran, but please call me Molly."

"M-Mary?" I stuttered. I stared at the girl, who smiled and held out her hand to shake. She was waiting for me.

"Are you all right?" she asked. "You look as if you've seen a ghost."

I stared back at my grandmother. "Oh, no," I said. "No. I think I'm just—hungry. You said something about . . . muffins?"

• 4 •

WHAT PARENTS DO

Now," Molly said, climbing down from the bed, "if you're going to stay, we should find you something to wear, don't you think?"

I nodded, stunned into silence. This girl was my grandmother? This laughing, pretty girl was going to grow up to be—*that*? It didn't make any sense.

"What color do you like best?" she called out from the closet. "Blue? Green?"

"Pink," I said. "I like pink."

Molly stuck her head back out at me, smiling. "That's my favorite too!" She reached for a pink dress, then walked back over to the bed and laid it out, along with socks and shoes, and some weird baggy underwear.

In the time it took me to undo my buttons, Molly had stepped out of her own nightgown and pulled a bright red dress over her head. Her curls popped up through the collar as she quickly zipped the side of the dress closed. "Ta-da!" she said, spinning around. "I win."

"No fair," I said. "I didn't even know we were racing. Plus, it's not what I'm used to, all these buttons."

"Oh, here, let me help you," said Molly. As I managed to get my arms into the sleeves, she began to button me up the back. "Tell me, what do future clothes look like? Are they silver? Do they help you fly?"

I laughed. "Nope, no flying. I wish." I looked down at my pink dress, which was crisply ironed and smelled like soap. It was something I might have worn in kindergarten for the school Easter parade. "Our clothes aren't so different, just stretchier, and girls wear pants a lot."

"Pants?" Molly's voice was shocked. "In *what* year?"

"In 1987," I said. "Am I done?" I turned to face her. "How do I look?"

Molly shook her head, amazed. "Pants . . . 1987," she repeated. Then, for no clear reason, she reached out and tickled me. "Got you!"

"Hey!" I yelped. "Stop!" I jumped away from her and

nearly fell over. "Cut that out! I hate it. The last person who tickled me was a kid named Reuben Meyer. I punched *him* in the gut."

"Oh," said Molly. She put her hands behind her back. "I thought it would be funny."

I straightened my dress. "It's not, but I'll forgive you. Just don't do it again. Okay?"

Molly nodded. "I'm sorry. It's just . . . my sisters have been gone for quite some time now."

"How is *that* an excuse for tickling someone you barely know?" I asked.

"I only meant . . . I'm not used to having actual people about, and it's very hard to upset imaginary friends. Would you *really* punch me?"

"*Probably* not," I admitted. "But why are you alone so much of the time?"

Molly sat down on the bed. "Mother took Ginny and Maggie away. To Pittsburgh, for a wedding, for the whole summer. I couldn't go because I've been ill, and Papa is busy, so I'm alone."

"Still, you can go out, can't you? To see friends? Now that you're better?"

Molly squirmed. "My parents worry. They like for me to be *careful*."

"Well, sure. That's what parents do. They're always

trying to protect you. They want to know where you're going, and they make you wear dumb raincoats and carry money for the pay phone, just in case. It's so annoying."

Molly shook her head. "You don't understand. It's not raincoats. Not for me. I was very sick." She paused theatrically and whispered, "I could *die*."

"Well, sure," I said. "Everyone could die."

"No. That's not what I mean," she said, shaking her head. "Or it is, but—oh, I don't know. It's different for me."

"What do you mean? Different how?"

"I mean . . . my parents are *very* careful. They don't like for me to leave."

"Don't like for you to leave where?"

"Here." She looked around the room.

"Here? You mean, you stay in this room all the time? Alone?"

"I have a sitting room," Molly said, gesturing at the door, "and a bathroom. But yes, this is my—my Lonely Room." She said this like a Lonely Room was a dining room. Like it was a normal thing.

"Lonely Room?" I asked.

Molly sat up higher on her knees. "My sister Ginny named it that. She and Maggie visit every day, when they're home. You see, I have asthma, and it's been much worse since I caught influenza. That's why I couldn't go to the wedding."

"Still, they went off and *left* you? Your whole family? For the *entire* summer?"

Molly shrugged.

"Well, you don't seem sick now," I said.

"I *am* better . . . that's true. The asthma comes and goes."

I nodded. "I know. I have asthma too. Of course, we have medicine, in the future, for stuff like that. But I know how it feels. Ugh. It's the worst."

"Medicine, for asthma?" Molly looked amazed. "That's better than silver flying suits."

"I guess so," I said. I glanced out the window. "I wonder, what do you do all day, sitting in here with nobody to talk to?"

"I have a radio!" Molly said. "It talks to me. I have loads of books. And Nora comes with my meals. Speaking of which, she could be here any minute. Let's go wash our teeth."

As I walked from the room, the thin white socks Molly had given me slid down into my Mary Janes. I stopped to tug them up, then looked around. Everything in the sitting room was different. There were walls in different places and the kitchen was missing. At the center of the room were a maroon brocade couch and a low table. A big wooden radio sat against one wall, flanked by bookshelves. I walked over to read the spines of the books but only recognized a few. *The Cuckoo Clock . . . East o' the Sun and West o' the Moon . . . Roller Skates . . .* I reached for a copy of *The Secret Garden—the* copy, I supposed. "At least I've read this one," I said.

"Oh, that's my very favorite," said Molly. "I've read it five times."

"*Five?*"

"It's special," she said. "Mother gave it to me." She pointed to a row of well-dressed dolls sitting on the floor against a wall. "And these are from Papa."

"Funny, I have one exactly like this," I said, crouching down to stroke the golden hair on one doll in particular.

"You do?" said Molly. "That's Arabella."

"Mine's named Junebug," I said, noticing a familiar scratch on the doll's arm. "She belonged to my mom. But I don't really play with her anymore. I haven't for years."

"Oh, me neither," said Molly. Then we both grinned and I could tell she was lying too.

"Over here is the bathroom," Molly said as she continued across the room. I followed her into an expanse of shining sea-green tile. Silver fixtures gleamed on a high sink. "Do you want to share?" said Molly, holding out a toothbrush with dark bristles that looked as if they might be actual hairs.

"Eh, no thanks," I said. "I'll use my finger to, umm, *wash* my teeth."

"Is that how it's done in the future?" Molly asked. She squirted a thick line of goop onto her brush and began to scrub ferociously.

I read the tube. The label said it would be *Double-Quick*. It also claimed to be delicious, but when I put a little on my finger and touched it to my tongue, I couldn't help making a face. There were bubbles in my mouth, actual soapsuds. *Blech*. I missed my Aquafresh.

When I was finished rinsing, I reached for a stiff-bristled wooden brush on the edge of the sink and attempted to pull it through my hair, which still had snarls in it from the windy car ride the night before. "Ouch!" I winced.

"Here, let me," said Molly. Before I could say anything else, she was pushing my shoulders down. I perched on the toilet seat as Molly brushed my hair and then braided it in quick, surprisingly gentle strokes until I had one perfect braid down my back.

"Nice!" I said, standing to look in the mirror. "Now it's your turn. Sit!"

"Really?" She touched her hair. "You don't have to. It musses again right away." She shook her curls. "See?"

"It's only fair," I said. "Sit."

Molly sat as I wet my hands and then finger-combed her curls until they hung in corkscrews. I added a little bit of lotion I found. It said LEMON VERBENA and smelled nice. I twisted some gently into each curl until it shone. Then I pulled all of Molly's hair up into a high side ponytail and tied a ribbon around it tightly, so that it stuck straight out. "Cute!" I said.

"What?" Molly turned her head sharply, so that the ponytail bounced. "Oh my, it feels funny!" She stood up and examined herself in the mirror. "Is this how people wear their hair in the future?" She batted at the bouquet of curls and leaned in for a closer look. "Lopsided?"

"Not *everyone*," I admitted. "But Valley Girls do. And rock stars. It's cool. You just need some dangly earrings."

"Rock stars," Molly asked, staring at herself. "What's a rock . . . ?"

Just then we heard a key turn in the lock.

"Nora!" mouthed Molly, looking back at me.

"Nora . . . ," I repeated. I set down the brush.

"Don't fret," Molly hissed. "I have a plan. Follow me."

We walked back into the sitting room just as a maid

came in, a tall girl in a black dress and white apron, with a white cap on her head. She was carrying a tray on one arm, so she could close the door with the other. When she saw me, her mouth dropped open. She set the tray on the coffee table, brushed her hands against her apron, and looked at Molly.

"Miss?" she said. "I'm afraid I don't understand—"

"My hair?" Molly said, reaching up to touch her burst of curls. "It's . . . new."

"No, miss," said the maid. "Not your hair." She jerked her head in my direction. "Your company!"

"Oh," said Molly. "*Oh!* This is Annie. She's visiting. Isn't that nice?"

Nora took a deep breath. "Miss, you know you aren't to have visitors. Doctor's orders. Your father said—"

"Please?" Molly pleaded. "Just this once?"

So far Molly's plan wasn't much of a plan, and it wasn't working.

Nora shook her head. "She'll have to leave, miss. I *am* sorry."

"But I'm always by myself," said Molly, slumping. "Always."

For a second I thought Nora might change her mind. Then she shook her head again. "I'll see her out, miss.

And I'll speak with your father about guests. You've been much stronger lately. Perhaps, if the doctor agrees, she might come for an hour, in the afternoon—"

Suddenly Molly's posture changed. She straightened up and put both fists on her hips. When she spoke, her voice was rigid, scolding. "In that case, Nora, maybe you shouldn't have been so careless as to leave the door unlocked last night!"

I stared at Molly. She didn't sound like herself. Was *this* her plan?

Nora was staring too. "But I never did—" she said defensively. "Why, I just now—" She held out her ring of keys.

Molly continued. "Luckily, Annie has turned out to be nice. But she could have been anyone, a thief! We don't want *Papa* to hear about this, do we?"

Nora stepped back a pace and folded her hands in front of her apron. She leaned against the door. "Why, miss—" she said.

"Poor Annie's an orphan," lied Molly. "An orphan with nowhere to go. Last night she snuck into the hotel and found my door open. She came in to escape the rain."

"But"—Nora looked at the key in her hand—"but, miss, I'm *sure* it wasn't open. Why, I just unlocked it this minute. Didn't you hear the key?"

It was true. I'd heard it turn in the lock myself. But Molly didn't seem bothered by this pesky fact.

"Then how did Annie get in here, do you think?" she asked the maid. "If *you* didn't leave the door unlocked."

"I'm sure I don't know," said Nora, shaking her head.

"You're the only person with a key. You *must* have left it open."

"I never did!"

Molly drew herself up until she was standing on tiptoe. The glare she shot the maid was almost cruel. "It doesn't much matter, does it?" she said. "What do you think Papa will do, Nora? What will happen to you if I tell him this story? It would really be a shame to lose you." Molly's eyes got squinty as she finished her speech, and it made me nervous. It was like I could see my witchy old grandmother peeking out.

Nora pursed her lips, gave a slight bob of the head, and said as she turned to leave, "All right, miss. Just as you say. I'll fetch your dishes when I bring lunch, like usual." Nora slipped away through the door and pulled it behind her. The key turned in the lock.

·5·

SPEAKING OF *THE SECRET GARDEN*

The minute the door closed, Molly flashed me a guilty smile and shrugged. "Thank goodness *that's* over." She sat down on the rug in front of her breakfast tray and started to deal out the cards. "Do you know how to play rummy?"

"I—yeah, of course," I said, dropping to my knees beside her.

"Oh, good!"

I watched Molly reach for the silver dome on her plate, lift it up, and sniff. She handed me a piece of toast.

"No muffins after all. But mmmm . . . scrapple! And marmalade, my favorite!"

"Ooh, mine too," I said, reaching for the jam jar. Just the sight of the oranges painted on the label made my mouth water.

Molly smiled. "Isn't it funny? Marmalade, asthma, *The Secret Garden*! We *do* have a lot in common." She reached for her juice glass. "You're more like me than my own sisters!"

I took a bite of my toast and chewed. "Hey," I said, "speaking of *The Secret Garden* . . ."

"Yes?" Molly cut up a piece of the gray mystery meat I had to assume was scrapple. "What about it?"

I set down my toast. "Why did you have to go all Mistress Mary on your maid just now?"

"Mistress Mary?" Molly looked confused. "I tried to be nice . . . at first. But she didn't give me a choice. Anyway, I wasn't *that* mean."

"You were *totally* mean. Bossing her like some lowly servant, like your ayah. It was *just* like in the book."

Molly looked thoughtful. "Well, she *is* a servant. Papa always says you have to be firm with them or—" Then it was as if Molly could hear the words tumbling out of her mouth. Her face changed. "Oh!" she said, blushing. "Oh, I *do* see what you're saying. It *is* like the book. I guess

I've never thought about it that way. That's—not good. I don't want to be Mary at the beginning. I want to be Mary *at the end*!" She looked upset.

"Yeah, well," I said, "I'm not trying to be some Goody Two-shoes, and I appreciate that you were trying to help me."

"I was!" she said. "Nora was going to make you leave. I had to do something, or you'd have been out in the streets."

"I guess . . . that's true," I said. "Still, she was only following your dad's orders."

A wave of hurt crossed Molly's face. "That's *all* she does, follow orders. She never stays to play or chat. She treats me like a chore."

"Well," I said, "you *are* a chore, kind of. You're her job, right?"

"Even so . . ."

"Sorry," I said, standing up. "I guess it isn't really my business. Anyway, nature calls. I'll be back in a sec."

Molly didn't look up as I headed to the bathroom, where I wrestled with my voluminous underpants and the scratchiest toilet paper in the history of the world. But as I was washing my hands, I noticed a breeze from behind the shower curtain. I pushed the curtain back and climbed into the claw-foot tub to stare through the open window.

Looking up, I noticed a church spire, but just below the window was something even better—a fire escape. It was a long way down to the footpath below, but there was a railing that ran the whole way.

I felt the hairs on my arms rise. Off in the distance, a car horn shouted *a-hoo-ha, a-hoo-ha*, as if to remind me that the world was still out there, waiting.

Back in the sitting room, Molly was chewing a fingernail intently. When I sat down, she pointed at her plate. "Do you want the last piece of scrapple? I saved it for you."

I shook my head. "I don't think so. What *is* scrapple, anyway?"

"Meat," said Molly.

I poked at the scrapple. It had lumps in it. "What kind of meat?"

"I'm not certain. Just . . . meat. Don't you eat scrapple in the future?"

"I eat mostly Lucky Charms for breakfast," I explained.

"Lucky Charms?"

"It's a cereal."

"Like cornflakes?"

"But with marshmallows."

"Marshmallows, for breakfast?" Molly looked amazed. "The future sounds miraculous."

I finished my toast and jam as we played a game of rummy and listened to the radio. It was nothing like the Top 40 countdown on Z93 back home. First there were church sounds—loud voices yelling about the throne of the Almighty, God the Fatherrrrrr, and President Roosevelt. Then there was a short soap opera, in which everyone sounded vaguely British and I had no idea what was happening. Something about a woman who'd gone around town without her stockings on.

Molly won the first game and dealt the cards again. As we started over, music came on the radio, jazzy orchestra stuff. Molly and I chewed our nails and concentrated on the cards. In the end, she won the second game too.

"Shall we play once more?" she asked, shuffling.

"I guess if you really want to beat me again," I said, stretching. "If that's fun for you."

Molly pointed to a stack of games under the coffee table. "We can play something else if you'd rather," she said. "Checkers?"

I peered at the boxes. Some games I recognized, like backgammon and Monopoly. Some I'd never seen before. "Whoa," I said, reaching for a box. "What's

British Empire: Trading with the Colonies? This looks hilarious."

"I haven't played that in a long time. It's not good to play alone." Molly opened the box. "Anyway, there are pieces missing. See?"

"That's okay," I said. "Maybe, instead of playing games, we could do something else."

"Like what?"

"Like . . . maybe we could go out?"

Molly put the lid back on the British Empire game. "You know I can't," she said quickly. "I mean, *we* can't. The door is locked."

"Right, but who needs a door, when we've got our own private fire escape?"

Molly shook her head. "It's too dangerous," she said.

"It looks pretty sturdy to me."

"It's not safe," Molly said sharply. "Even if we make it all the way down, I could have an attack. I could die out there."

"But you won't . . ."

"You can't know that," said Molly.

"Yes, I can!" The words slipped out before I knew what I was doing.

Molly stared at me. "How can you possibly be sure of that?" she asked.

I didn't know what to say.

Then it dawned on her. I could see it, like in cartoons when a lightbulb goes off over someone's head. "Wait," she said, getting excited. "Wait, wait, *wait*! If you're from the future . . . you know what *happens*. . . ."

What had I done? I blinked. I shrugged in what I hoped was a vague and mysterious way. I reached for the deck of cards again. "Forget it. Let's play rummy," I said.

Molly shouted. "You *do* know what happens to me!"

"N-no, I don't," I stammered. "I mean, hardly anything. Really."

She rose up on her knees. "Whatever you do know, you have to tell me!"

I pushed away a fleeting thought of a woman in a bed, a shrill angry voice, six whiskers. "Really, Molly! I don't know anything more. I swear."

Molly frowned. "Truly?"

"Truly," I lied softly. "But . . ."

"But?"

"I can promise you this much," I said. "You have a lot of boring years ahead of you, if you just sit around, playing rummy. Come on!" I said. I stood up and grabbed at her hand. I pulled her to her feet, and she let herself be pulled. I tugged her arm and led her into the bathroom, over to the window.

"Look," I said, pointing. "Look at all that sunshine. Wouldn't you like to be out in it?"

She nodded slowly, cautiously.

"And hey, I'll go first. If I'm wrong and I fall to my death, you can scrape me off the street and make that scrapple stuff out of me. How's *that* for a silver lining?"

Molly wrinkled her nose. "I don't suppose you'd taste very good."

"Ha," I said. "Very funny."

Molly walked over to the tub, climbed in, and stared out the open window. When she glanced back over her shoulder at me, her eyes were misty, and her mouth was twitching. It was like her feelings were fighting with each other.

"Oh, Molly, please?" I begged. "Pretty, pretty please? I don't know how long I *have*. I could be back here in an hour. I don't want to waste the magic. I want to do things, see things!"

"All right!" she said at last. "All right. Let's do things. Let's see things!"

"Really?" I said.

"Really."

"Awesome!"

"Yes," she said. Then she repeated after me, "Awe-*some*!"

Unfortunately, at that moment we heard a key turn in the lock. Nora was back. As we dashed back into the sitting room and took our spots at the low table, Nora silently brought in bowls of chicken noodle soup and glasses of cold milk. She set everything on the table before us and collected the breakfast dishes carefully.

Molly didn't say a word. Neither did Nora. I arranged my napkin in my lap.

"Thanks," I called out as cheerfully as I could. "This looks great."

Nora dropped a stiff curtsy. "You're quite welcome, I'm sure."

Beside me, Molly cleared her throat. "Yes, umm, thank you, Nora," she said, "for your hard work. I don't say thank you enough."

Nora blinked at me, and then looked back to Molly. "You're certainly welcome as well, miss," she said. "Happy to be of service."

As Nora reached for the doorknob, Molly spoke again. "Nora, one more thing?"

The maid turned. "Yes, miss?"

"It's just—"

Nora paused by the door.

Molly examined her soup, blushing. "I'm—I'm sorry

for the way I spoke to you earlier. I wouldn't actually do . . . that thing I said."

Nora stared at Molly. Her face was soft. When she spoke, her voice was gentle. "It's all right, miss. Don't you fret. You've got enough to worry about without thinking of me, dear."

Molly jerked her head up in surprise at the word *dear*, but she didn't say anything, and Nora was already through the door with the breakfast dishes.

"Good job," I said.

She replied by turning away from me and slurping her soup.

When we were done, she pointed at my bowl. "You aren't fond of mushrooms either?" she asked.

I looked down at the two bowls, side by side, full of mushroom slivers. I shook my head. "Squishy and awful. No." I stuck my tongue out.

"It's uncanny," said Molly, "how much we have in common. It really is."

· 6 ·

SITTING IN THE SKY

At first it was enough just to be sitting in the sky. Side by side, we gazed at the blue overhead, at the tall trees waving from the yard below. I could feel the metal grid of the sunbaked fire escape through my cotton dress.

"You know, this isn't the first time I've done this," said Molly. "I *used* to come out here."

"Why'd you stop? It's so nice."

"That was when my sisters were home. We'd all climb out together, to watch the birds. Sometimes we'd picnic. It's different alone."

"Molly," I said, "how long *have* you been alone?"

"Twenty-seven days. But it feels longer."

"I bet! But your dad is still here, right?"

"Oh, yes," she said. "There's Papa, sometimes."

"And how long will your sisters and your mom be away?"

She shrugged. "Not much longer, I hope."

"What about before that? You said your sisters came out here with you. Does that mean you were locked up *before* they went away? How long have you been here altogether?"

She tilted her head, thinking hard. "I'm not exactly certain. I had influenza at Christmas, but not *last* Christmas."

"Oh," I said. "Wow." A year and a half, locked up. It sounded crazy-making.

Without warning, the church bells next door rang out and we clapped our hands to our ears. As they faded, I noticed other noises, so different from the sounds of home. Clips and clops, putters and shouts.

"It's pretty," I said.

"It's dirty." Molly wrinkled her nose.

"That too. Pretty *and* dirty." I stared out at the stained slate rooftops, the gray brick streets. Dingy smoke drifted in the air. But I also detected a faint whiff of cinnamon again.

"Do you smell that?" I asked.

Molly took a deep breath. "I do," she said. "That happens some days. But I don't know what it is."

"At home, it never smells like that," I said.

"Where *is* home?" asked Molly. "You haven't said."

"Atlanta," I told her. "Georgia."

"Atlanta," she repeated wistfully. "In the south. Magnolias. Peaches. I'd like to go there. Tell me something about it, your Atlanta, in the future."

Part of me wanted to tell her that in the future, parents got arrested for locking their kids in rooms for days on end. Instead I said, "Well, hmm . . . there's TV. It's like . . . movies, but on little screens, in your house. All day long."

"Movies? In your house?" Molly looked amazed. "How do people ever stop watching?"

I laughed, thinking of my soap opera–addicted neighbor, Mrs. Bobby. "Some don't."

Suddenly Molly stood up and pointed. "I know! If we're really going to climb down, maybe we can go *there*."

"Where?" I stood up beside her, trying to see what she was pointing at.

"See, out there, that gray line in the distance? That's the harbor. It leads to the bay. And *that* leads to the ocean."

"Man, I love the beach," I said. "Don't you?"

Molly didn't respond. When I turned to look at her, I saw that her lashes sparkled with tears.

"Whoa!" I said. "You okay?"

A few drops fell as Molly smiled. They left dark spots on her red dress. "Yes," she said. "I'm happy."

"Then why are you crying?"

She took a deep breath. "It's just so much. The wind. The sun. You. Please don't think I'm a ninny. I've just been sitting so long, imagining the fun things Maggie and Ginny were doing, trying not to hate them. I've been so alone. But now *you're* here, and I don't need to be jealous anymore. It feels . . . better."

"Hey, want to know something funny?" I said "When my mom is upset, she doesn't cry. She eats ice cream instead."

"Really? Does that help her?"

"Mom says you only get so many minutes alive. Why waste them crying?"

"Well, I *like* to cry. Sometimes." Molly turned to face the stairs. "But I think I'm done now. Are you ready?"

"Yep."

As I walked carefully down that first set of stairs, the metal shuddered under my feet. The wind that rustled the ivy beside me puffed out my skirt and threatened to blow it over my head. I ignored everything else and concentrated on the narrow walkway under my slippy shoes. I'd climbed plenty of jungle gyms in my life, but they weren't a hundred feet tall, and I had always had sneakers on. I gripped the railing. One staircase. Two staircases. All the way down.

At last I hit sturdy ground. My knees felt wobbly. I glanced around, then ducked behind a hedge.

When Molly joined me in the prickly hedge, her eyes were wide. "I did it!" she whisper-shouted in my ear. "I can't imagine what Papa will say if he catches me, but just now I don't care!" She laughed. "I'm still breathing, aren't I?"

"It would be pretty hard to ask that if you weren't."

Molly giggled. "*Now* what?"

"You tell me," I said. "This is your town."

"No," she said. "You decide. This was *your* idea."

"Well, you said you wanted to go to the harbor. How do we get there?"

Molly shrugged her thin shoulders. "I haven't the faintest idea."

"Well then, what are some other cool 1937 things? What have you missed, being stuck in your tower for the last year and a half? Where did you like to go before you got the flu?"

Molly blushed. "Oh. You still don't understand."

"Understand *what?*"

"Annie, I've *always* been sick. I've *always* had asthma. They've kept me inside so that I wouldn't catch anything. My lungs are weak and . . ."

"Wait, you mean before you got the flu? *Before* the Lonely Room?"

She nodded.

"So all your life, you've never gone *anywhere?*"

"I go to church sometimes, there." She motioned up at the spire.

"What about school?" I asked.

"I have a tutor," she murmured. "During the school year. Miss Tompkins."

"Wow," I said. "Wow."

"It's never been like *this* before," Molly explained. "Until the Lonely Room, I lived with the others, on the second floor. I could walk in the garden. Read in the lobby. Other children came to stay in the hotel, and I talked to them. It wasn't so bad. Truly."

"It sounds *crazy,*" I said, shaking my head. "I mean—you look *fine.* I have asthma too, and nobody ever locked me up! You just ran down this entire building, seven floors. Don't you think maybe your parents are wrong? That the doctor made a mistake? That you're better?"

"I'd *like* to believe that," said Molly. "But I'd like to believe a lot of things."

"Well, if *you* don't know where to go, and *I* don't know where to go, then we might as well go"—I held out a finger and pointed randomly from my spot behind the hedge—"*that* way!"

Molly peered out cautiously. After a second she nodded. I stood up, ducked out from behind the hedge, and began to run as fast as I could. Behind me I heard Molly's shoes thudding in the grass too.

Our dash took us into the alley that curved away from the hotel and ran behind a row of houses. At last I bent over, a stitch in my side. Molly arrived a second later, wheezing slightly.

"You okay?" I asked, trying to straighten up.

With a hand on her chest, Molly flashed a huge grin. "I *am*!" she panted. "I did it . . . I *ran*! I can't remember . . . the last time I did. I'm not sure . . . I *ever* did."

"That's great," I said, "but maybe let's walk a bit." I winced, holding my side.

Molly was still panting, but she beamed. "Walking," she said, "is good . . . too."

Once we caught our breath, it was nice in the sun-filled alley. We kicked pebbles and tried to ignore the stink of trash, which spilled from cans everywhere. I looked over at Molly, happily shuffling her shoes in the dust. The alley ran between two rows of narrow houses, whose backyards were only little strips of grass about ten feet wide, separated by low fences. In a few places, women were out, with mouths full of clothespins, hanging up laundry. They waved at us as we went by. We waved back.

Just as we came to the end of the alley, a horse trotted up behind us and turned into the street beyond. Molly and I both jumped when the animal snorted and moved past us, pulling a black-and-red wagon full of vegetables. We watched horse and wagon rattle away up the street, a jostle of color, as a man's voice, loud and deep and strong like a train whistle, sang out, "Berrrrries, berrrrries, got yer berrrrrries. Cherrrrrrries, cherrrrrries, got yer cherrrrries. Come on, all you pretty Marrrrrrrys!"

"What's *that*?" I said, staring after him.

"He's an arabber," said Molly. "Don't you have those in Atlanta?"

I shook my head. "A what?"

"An arabber," said Molly. "They live with their horses in the stables and work in the streets. They come to the kitchen to sell things to Cook. Instead of knocking on the door, they sing down the alley. Cook comes out when she hears the song. Especially if it's a man named Russell.

I think she likes him." Molly giggled. "Sometimes, before the Lonely Room, I'd run down if I heard him coming, and he'd give me a banana."

After that, we turned left and walked after the arabber and his song. Block by block, the street got busier. People moved past us in a hurry. On one corner, we had to step over two boys sharing a comic book in the middle of the sidewalk. Up and down the street, women were out in the sun with scarves tied around their heads, kneeling on the tiny marble stoops of their row houses with pails. Each had a scrub brush and was ferociously attacking the steps leading to her door.

"Are they having a contest, do you think?" I asked Molly. "How do they all know to come out at the same time?"

"I suppose it's just wash day." Molly shrugged.

"Wow, I've never seen Mom scrub anything like that. Never." I tried to imagine it: Mom out on the porch, scouring the Georgia red clay off the steps. I could hear her voice in my head: "I'll show you where you can stick your scrub brush!"

"Is the future filthy, then?" asked Molly.

"I don't *think* so," I said. "If it is, I never noticed. Maybe we just balance everything out by not having horse poop everywhere." I pointed to a particularly huge pile as I said this. I wrinkled my nose.

"Then where *do* the horses . . . *poop*?" asked Molly.

"We don't *have* horses," I said.

Molly considered that. "Where did they all go? The horses?"

"I don't know," I said. "Maybe Texas?"

We turned a corner and a sky-blue streetcar rumbled past as a man ran to catch it. Molly grabbed my arm and linked it with hers. "Let's not lose each other," she said. Now the houses gave way to storefronts, and the shop windows were full of prices I couldn't believe for things I'd never heard of. What was a *spat*? I wondered. What was *hair dressing*?

We passed a shoeshine man and a woman selling flowers. On the corner across the street, two police officers in blue uniforms were laughing. A few blocks after that, I stopped in front of a huge window and a bright red sign that read F. W. WOOLWORTH CO. "Now *here's* something that hasn't changed!"

"Really?" said Molly. "What do they sell here?"

"Everything, pretty much!" I said.

"I like everything," said Molly as she pushed the door open. "I think."

• 7 •

ALMOST LIKE I BELONG

I followed Molly into the store. "They don't really have *everything*. It's just a five-and-dime, but Mom and I like it. On Saturdays we eat grilled cheese at the counter, then try on jewelry and stuff."

"That sounds nice," said Molly, staring around.

I inhaled deeply. The confused scent of candy and baby powder and rubber gloves and hamburgers made me homesick and happy. "It *is* nice," I said. "That's exactly what it is." Though *nice* wasn't what I'd have expected from a magical adventure, it made me smile. "Never mind

Camelot." I laughed. "*I* traveled back in time to take my grandma to Woolworth's."

"Pardon?" asked Molly, turning to look over her shoulder.

"Oh, umm, nothing. Nothing important."

Just inside the front door, a bunch of kids were huddled together around the outside of a photo booth.

"What's *that*?" asked Molly, joining their throng.

Squeals of laughter came from inside the booth, where a voice shouted, "Hey, cut that!" One second later a small boy in a dark suit and cap shot out from behind the curtain. Just behind him, a taller, older boy snorted with laughter. Molly studied the kids carefully. When at last the small strip of photographs shot into the small boy's hand, the crowd wandered off.

Molly didn't budge. "I want to do it," she said. She grabbed my hand and pulled me inside the booth.

"Ack, wait," I said. "My braid is all messy! And you need money."

Molly conjured a coin from somewhere and slipped it into the slot with a heavy *shick*, then a light flashed. I looked up, blinked. The light flashed again and I smiled this time, leaned in to touch heads with Molly. Unexpectedly she turned and threw an arm around me, squeezing hard. I laughed, and without thinking I hugged her back, felt her ribs in my arms, her curls on my cheek.

It was only while we were waiting for our pictures that I remembered the last time I'd done this, with Susie at the mall, the two of us in the arcade, sticking out our tongues, giving each other rabbit ears. We'd pretended to make out with ourselves, our own arms wrapped around our chests, backs to the camera, hands groping our necks. Wow, we were goofs.

When the pictures fell into Molly's hand, slightly shiny and wet, my own face staring out at me looked unfamiliar. In black-and-white, with the braid and round collar, I looked like a stranger. Molly and I were just two faces, girls who might have been sisters, in nearly identical dresses.

"Hey," I said, "I look almost like I belong here."

Molly was cupping the strip of photos in her hands and blowing on it, as she'd seen the boys do. "And I," she whispered, "look like—*you!*"

"Nah!" I said quickly. "You're crazy. Come on, let's look around."

We headed deeper into the store, and I had to admit to myself that things were different after all. Instead of counters, the room was full of big tables, and everything was pretty much just heaped on top of them. I stopped in front of a pile of pink parasols and fake flowers and music boxes. The sign above my head read NOTIONS DEPARTMENT.

"Can I help you, young ladies?" asked a nervous-looking man who appeared out of nowhere.

"Oh, no," I replied as Molly wandered off into the ribbon department. "Just window-shopping."

"Well, if you need help with something in particular, something you'd *actually* like to purchase, do let me know."

"Okay!" I said, walking away. I could feel his eyes on my back, and when I turned my head, he was still standing there, his arms crossed over his chest. "Thanks!" I called out. "See you around!" I hurried away.

When I found Molly, she was wearing a paper party hat covered in feathers. There was a thick strand of tinsel around her neck.

"Doing some shopping?" I asked. "That's a good look for you."

"I'm afraid not," she answered with a deep sigh. "I didn't bring my money, really. I just had that one quarter in my pocket, my lucky piece. Perhaps we can come back? Tomorrow?"

"Sure," I said. "If I'm still here. But let's not stay too long today. That guy is stalking us." I jerked my head in the direction of the nervous man, who was now staring at us over an armload of boxes. I waved at him and he turned away, headed for the back of the room.

"Five more minutes?" Molly asked, reaching for a perfume bottle.

"Sure," I said, coughing as she sprayed everything in sight.

I ran from the smell of the perfume, to the front of the store, where I stopped to examine a tray of candy bars. Some sounded awesome, like the Chocolate Ice Cubes and the Milk Shake Bars. But the Chicken Dinner Bar? Blech. Even for a penny, I'd be afraid to try that one.

I moved over to a table covered with beautiful painted glass lamp shades. They were all different colors, arranged in a carefully balanced pyramid. The Woolworth's back home didn't sell things like that. It was more full of flip-flops and coat hangers.

I was kneeling to examine the pictures painted on the shades, when across the room I heard a voice call out sharply, "Miss, no, don't—OH, NO, MISS!"

I whirled around to see what the trouble was and found a blurred rush of color heading straight at me. It flew through the store, down the aisle. Fast!

I heard: "*Aaaaaaannieee!!!*" Molly was flying at me, zipping along the dark wooden floors, still in her feather hat, and she wasn't slowing down! The nervous man ran behind her, but his arms were full of boxes and Molly was zooming. She sped forward, windmilling, screaming. "*Ayyyyyyy!*"

I threw my hands up to catch her, or stop her, or at least brace myself. It was all I had time for. I squinted my eyes and gritted my teeth and—*BANG!* She hit me like a freight train. I caught myself against the table and took a sharp corner in my hip. Molly grabbed my neck with both arms, and we toppled heavily against the table but didn't hit the floor.

Then I looked at the pyramid of lamp shades. . . .

For a second or two it was a tremble, a shudder, a shiver, like a bowling pin that *might* tip if you wait. The stack of bright jewel-colored lamps, shining in the afternoon sun, wobbling. I held my breath.

The lamps slipped. They fell like a house of cards. It was beautiful, explosive. One, then another, until *BOOMCRASH!* They hit the table, then the floor, shattered into glitter beside us. Molly and I stood frozen as shards splintered all around our feet. Colors everywhere.

Molly let go of my neck, straightened herself up, then grabbed my arm with one hand and the table with the other. When I looked at her feet, I understood.

"Roller skates?" I asked.

"Oops?" she said.

In slow motion, the nervous man arrived, a look of horror on his face. He kept his distance at first, maybe afraid of the sharp bits and splinters. Maybe afraid of Molly, that she might roll again.

From the back of the store, a saleswoman with a bright red mouth skittered out in heels. "Can I help? Is everyone all right?"

The nervous man didn't answer. He looked astounded, adrift.

"Oh my," said the woman, her red mouth forming a vivid O.

Molly only pulled off her feather hat and said softly, "Annie?" as though I'd know what to do.

I took it all in. The damage. The man, who was now beginning to stutter something. The fact that we didn't have a penny between us, that Molly was not supposed to be out of the Lonely Room, and that I wasn't supposed to exist. This was bad.

I stared into Molly's face, so close to mine. "Can you run?"

Her fingers dug into my arm. "I don't know if—"

"*Can* you?"

She nodded faintly. "If you hold on to me."

"Do it," I hissed. "Go now. NOW!"

We bolted! Before anyone could ask any questions or

grab us. I pulled Molly after me, teetering wildly. The two of us made it through the glass shards and the front of the store, past the photo booth, to the doorway.

It took the nervous man a minute to realize what was happening. "No!" he shouted at last. When I looked behind me, he was hopping around, trying to avoid the glass. "You girls! Come back! No!" We could hear him shouting as we ran into the sun, then down the sidewalk.

We didn't stop. We kept going, running and rolling sloppily down the pavement. We knocked over a baffled woman walking a small dog. "Sorry!" I shouted as we passed. "Super sorry!"

Molly half skated, half walked, with a chunking sound, and I pulled at her as well as I could. I didn't look back again, so I didn't know if we were being chased. Blocks behind me I could still hear the man shouting, hollering. In the end, he only bothered with one word.

"Police!" he screamed, as we were swallowed by the crowd on the sidewalk. "Police police police police police!"

Then, out of nowhere, a dark tunnel appeared in the brick wall beside us, a narrow space, a doorway sliced between two row houses. I didn't know what it was, but I took a chance and ducked inside, pulling Molly with me. The tunnel stank. It was dark and narrow. The ceiling dripped.

We made it about twenty feet in the darkness, then collapsed onto a pile of what felt like wooden crates. "Sit," I wheezed at Molly. "Get . . . those . . . off!" I leaned over for a minute, hand to chest, to catch my breath.

"I—I didn't mean to," she stammered, tears in her voice. "It was my first time. I didn't know. . . ."

"Don't . . . cry. And don't . . . *worry*. Just get . . . those off."

Molly began to pull off the skates, which were clamped to her shoes. I could hear her fingers scrambling at the buckles. As each skate hit the ground, it made a clattery metal noise.

"Done," Molly said at last. "Done." She leaned against me. "I—only wanted to try them."

"I know," I said. I had caught my breath again. "And now you have. It's fine."

"Fine? It's not fine. All that glass? The *police*?" she said. "What will happen?"

As though in answer to our question, a police officer ran by the entrance to our tunnel at that very second, his club waving, his feet beating the pavement. He paused briefly to squint down our way. We held our breath, both of us. Silent.

"Anyone there?" he shouted into the darkness. "Hello?"

We waited, frozen.

At last he ran on ahead and I let out my breath, gasping painfully for air. Molly did the same. Then we stood up. "Okay," I said. "Now we scram. Home?"

"But—we stole the skates! And all those lamps broken! We have to go back."

I thought that over. "We will," I said. "When we have the money."

"But . . ."

"Look, we *can't* talk to the police. The minute they know who you are, they'll go to your dad for the cash."

"Oh," said Molly. "I hadn't thought about that. You're always right, aren't you?"

"Usually," I said.

Molly smothered a laugh.

I didn't want to pop back out into the street, where people were on the lookout for two girls in a hurry. So we headed the other way, back between the row houses, deeper into the tunnel, which grew narrower and danker. Beneath our feet the ground was sludgy.

Somewhere, something squeaked.

· 8 ·

THE REVOLTING TREASURE

Our tunnel ended in a splintery wooden door, but when we creaked it open, we found our way blocked by a clump of overgrown bushes. I squinted and pushed through the scratchy foliage. Molly followed, and we both stumbled into a small fenced yard.

Full of chickens!

The birds were as bewildered to see us as we were to see them. They jumped and rustled and clucked. Most of them ran to the other side of the small dirt patch. But one huge bird separated itself from the rest. Fearless, he flew at me, screaming. Screaming!

I froze.

Molly yelled, "AGHHHHH!"

The rooster turned when it heard her and charged. He jumped at Molly's head, squawking and scrambling his feet in the air.

"AGHHHHH!" Molly yelled again, hands over her head, body bent double as claws and feathers raked the air around her curls. The big bird leaped straight onto her head.

"AGHHHHH!" she screamed again as he ran down her back, flapping his wide wings. He stretched himself.

"Go, go, go!" I shouted at her. "Stand up! Run, Molly! MOVE!" I dashed over and waved my arms at the bird on her back. "GET!" I shouted at him. "SHOO!"

"BRAWK!" he shouted back, mouth open. He had lizard eyes.

"FRIED CHICKEN!" I bellowed, slapping at his chest. "EXTRA CRISPY!"

He screamed, "RAHHHHHHHHHHHH!"

Finally Molly shook herself and ran for the back of the yard. The rooster sprang away as she dashed, and the two of us pushed through the other birds. "MCNUGGETS!" I shouted as I ran, waving my arms and kicking my feet to keep the chickens off me. I pushed open the latch on the gate and we ran through.

We collapsed on the gravelly ground of an alley and leaned against a garage wall. Molly, pale and panting, looked over at me with the hugest eyes I'd ever seen. Her neck was scratched.

I couldn't help it. I started to laugh. Then I couldn't stop.

"It's not funny," Molly said. "That was horrible."

I only laughed louder. "Ha—ha—ATTACK CHICKEN!" I shouted.

She crossed her arms over her chest. "Well, it didn't scratch *you*, so you don't know how it felt. It *hurt*."

I wiped away a tear from laughing. "Heh. Sorry. It was pretty funny from where I was standing." I stood up and did an imitation of her, bent over, the chicken dancing on her back. "AGHHHHH!" I shouted.

Molly smiled.

Then she grinned.

I reached out a hand to pull her up. I looped my arm through hers as we walked down the alley. "*That*," I laughed, "was quite an afternoon. You sure made up for lost time."

Molly grimaced. "I feel terrible about the lamps."

"It was worth it for the crash." I grinned. "And you should have seen yourself on those skates."

"But, Annie, we *stole* them."

I shrugged. "We didn't *mean* to, and we'll pay for everything, right?"

Molly nodded slowly. "I suppose so," she said. "Yes, of course we will."

"Then it all works out," I said. "No reason to feel too bad. Okay?"

Molly didn't answer me. Instead she pointed to something behind my head. "Look at that," she said. "Now *that's* something to do!"

I turned and saw the sign:

SILVERQUEEN CARNIVAL AND FUN FAIR!
AUGUST 15–22!

The poster's writing was in orange and purple. It had a picture of a Ferris wheel and dancing girls. "Hey, neat!" I breathed. "See, things get better if you just wait a minute."

"That does seem to be true," said Molly. "We'll have to do that tomorrow, when we have some money!"

"But . . . ," I said, frowning, "tomorrow I might not be here. Can't we go home and get some money now?"

"It's getting late," said Molly. "And Nora will be coming with supper. In fact, we should really get home."

"I guess you're right," I grumbled.

Together we hustled along the alleys, making turns here and there, with our eyes on the church spire. We were almost home when Molly stopped and put a finger to her lips. "Hush!"

"What?" I listened but heard nothing.

Molly was standing still, with her hands out beside her like a doll. "Don't you hear it?" she hissed.

"No. And why are we whispering?" I hissed back.

"Shhh!" said Molly.

I stood there another minute as Molly walked in a circle, listening carefully at garage doors and trash cans, but I still had no clue what she'd heard. It was like she was entranced. Suddenly she gave a sharp cry and whipped the lid off a dented silvery can that had been set out in the alley. She gripped the lip of the can in both hands and tried to tip it over. It was too heavy.

"What are you doing?" I asked.

"Just help me," she said, panting. "Don't you hear that? It's awful. Oh, help!"

"Help *what*?" I asked. "I don't hear anything." Still, I began to tug at the other handle. It didn't budge. "What am I supposed to hear?"

In answer, Molly plunged her thin arms into the gross slop in the can and began hauling out fistfuls of trash. I gagged at the smell, but Molly didn't even seem to notice it as she reached for rotting potato peels that oozed through her fingers and old rags, soaked and stained. At last I could hear it too. A faint cry.

Molly leaned deeper into the can until her legs were dangling off the ground, and when she emerged, she was clutching what looked like a dead chipmunk. The chipmunk uncurled itself, squeaked, and turned into the smallest, skinniest, wettest, most pathetic kitten I'd ever seen.

Molly stared at the revolting treasure, and then up at me. Her eyes were huge and bright. She cradled the thing in her arms.

"Oh!" I said. "Oh, Molly." I reached out to pet the creature, with its pink translucent ears, its wet face like a skull, its shivering rib cage. "How did you hear it? How did you know?"

She stared at me. "How did you *not?*"

We walked the rest of the way along the alley and tiptoed up the fire escape stairs as cautiously as we could. Molly was in the lead this time, cradling the kitten in one arm and holding the railing with the other. She was climbing hundreds of feet into the air with gobs of trash sticking in her curls, but she didn't appear to notice. When we got to the top, she gave me the smelly handful of fur, which shivered and flinched at my touch. Molly crawled into the bathroom. I passed back her slimy bundle, then climbed in after her.

Tenderly Molly washed the kitten with a bar of soap lathered onto a washcloth. All the while she sang softly to the pitiful creature in a lullaby voice: "The way your smile just beams, the way you sing off-key, the way you haunt my dreams. No, no, they can't take that away from me. . . ." I didn't know the words, but it sounded familiar.

The kitten showed his appreciation by crying piteously and trembling the entire time, but Molly didn't look like she minded. At the end she washed the inside of his ears, muttering, "Ouch, I know, shhh," and wincing with his mews as though she was in pain.

Once he had been rubbed dry with a towel, the kitten shook himself out into a fluff ball and crawled onto Molly's shoulder. There he began to purr loudly. Dry, he turned out to be a sort of golden color, with big dark leopard spots and incredibly long whiskers. He looked half wild.

"You know, cats are bad for your asthma," I said.

Molly shook her head. "How could I care about that? Poor thing, in the dark, all alone. Just think what might have happened if the trash collector had come. But we found him, didn't we?"

Molly held the kitten up to her face and kissed his

tiny nose. "You'll stay with me, and I won't let anything hurt you, ever. *That's* a promise."

The kitten blinked his yellow eyes. He'd stopped purring.

Molly added, "Unless you don't *want* to stay, of course. I wouldn't keep you here if you didn't like it. You can come and go as you like. All right?"

As if he understood, the kitten squinched up his face at Molly. "Mew."

Molly and I cracked up. Our laughter echoed against the tile walls.

"You should call him Lucky," I said. "Because that's what he is, lucky."

Molly shook her head. "No, I'm going to call him Friend. Because he's that too."

Later, when we were in the bedroom with Friend and the light outside the window was fading, we heard Nora open the door. Molly set the sleeping kitten down on her pillow and crooked a finger at me. Quietly we left the room, closing the door on our secret. By the time we sat down, dinner was on the table.

"How was your afternoon, miss?" Nora asked politely.

Molly beamed, setting her napkin in her lap. "It was wonderful, Nora, really wonderful," she said. "How was *your* day?"

Nora looked startled, but then she smiled back and said easily, "Why, it was good enough, I suppose. Ordinary, but good enough. Kind of you to ask."

Molly nodded pleasantly.

"Thanks for dinner," I added.

"You're most welcome, miss."

I watched Nora move around the room. She set a tall glass of cloudy liquid on the side table for Molly and cleared the dishes. Then she waved goodbye.

Molly and I ate our dinner: chicken in a cream sauce. After a little while, Friend emerged, nudging the door open with a tiny paw. We fed him small bites of chicken, which he snapped up gently. After that we listened to music on the radio for a while, and though it was much earlier than I ever went to bed at home, the day felt done. Molly walked over to the glass of cloudy water and drank it down, gulping it all at once. She made a face.

"What's that?" I asked.

"Medicine," she said. "To help me sleep."

"Oh."

Molly began to look drowsy right away. When she stumbled into the bedroom, I followed. I didn't want her to fall down on the floor.

We changed into nightgowns, then climbed into bed. Molly lay with her eyes open, staring at me glassily. "I'm glad you're here," she said. "I didn't know it was you I was wishing for, but you were exactly what I wanted."

"I'm glad too," I said. My voice came out soft, whispery, just like Molly's.

"And I'm glad"—she yawned—"I'm glad we went outside. What a day! We just need to puzzle out the lamps." She yawned again, more deeply. "The morning. We'll think about it in the morning." She paused before adding, "It's funny, to have something to think about in the morning. I can't . . . remember . . . the last . . . time. . . ." Then she was asleep, whistling faintly through her nose.

I lay there awhile, staring at the canopy. I knew I probably wouldn't be here tomorrow for the fair. I wouldn't ever know if Molly paid for the lamps, or if she got to keep Friend. But if I was going to wake up in my own time, I wanted to take what memories I could with me, keep them. What a day it had been! I wanted to file each bit of it away. This place. *This* Molly, not the old woman Molly. How could they possibly be the same person? I turned my head to stare at her mop of curls.

I felt my eyes start to shut. I didn't *want* to fall asleep yet. I wasn't ready to be done. But it wasn't up to me. My eyes were closing, and the world was drifting. *I* was drifting.

• 9 •

GOING OUT TO COME IN AGAIN

I opened my eyes and felt fuzzy, almost exactly like when I got my tooth pulled and the dentist gave me silly gas. At first I just lay there in that big bed, staring up at the blurry canopy, trying to remember . . . *anything*.

Outside, steady rain beat on the window. Fingers drumming in my brain. What *was* it? What did I need to remember?

Then I felt something sharp in my hair. I turned over in my haze and saw a kitten and a dark mop of hair snoring just beyond it. I stared at the tangle of hair and the girl attached to it, trying to figure out who she was.

And who I was.

Who was *I*?

Memories began to float in, faintly, like ghosts. Vaguely, I remembered a horse, a glittery crash, running. Then I remembered an important word, *my* word: *Annie.* It was like I'd slipped free of my name and now I was putting it back on. *I'm Annie*, I thought. That felt better. I glanced over at the girl beside me, and I remembered: *Molly*. Each memory was like a star in a constellation. The picture was becoming clearer. I looked at my hands and they looked familiar.

Then, as if moving backward in time, I slid further—memories of the dark hotel, the smell of carnations. *Mom!* It all came together, the whole crazy story, and behind it, like a backdrop, *home*. My neighborhood. Susie. School. As though my real life were the farthest thing from me, and I had to reach for it.

The snoring girl beside me—Molly—felt more real. The room. The kitten purring, and the clean white sheets. Those things were here, in my now.

I squeezed my eyes shut, opened them again, and my vision felt clearer. Huh. I recalled Molly drinking the cloudy medicine, but I didn't think I'd drunk any.

Beside me, Molly stirred. "Ouch," she said. The kitten had climbed onto her chest and was licking her chin. She opened her eyes and then sat up brightly, clutching Friend. "You're here!" she said. "I thought perhaps I dreamed you."

"I'm here . . . ," I said, flustered. "Still here."

Molly looked so happy, but I felt . . . lost. Why hadn't I gone home? In books, magic always ended where it began, didn't it? You just had to walk back through the wardrobe. I'd climbed back into the huge bed that had brought me here, hadn't I?

I turned over. Was there something I was missing? A talisman, a magic thing? Or a trick I needed to know, something I was supposed to have done before bed? Words to repeat? *Open sesame! Alakazam!* I didn't think so. . . .

Then Molly was climbing out of bed, and it wasn't foggy-headed morning anymore. It was tomorrow. There were fresh clothes to put on (my new dress was brown, with tiny pink flowers), hair to braid, and teeth to wash. Everything moved quickly, more quickly than I did, in my sluggish state. Before I was ready, Nora arrived with breakfast.

Then I was eating. I was talking. I was taking my

hand of cards from Molly and sitting down at the table. Like everything would be fine.

Probably it would. Probably I just needed to stop worrying, have a good day, one more chance to see things. Hadn't I been happy for this adventure? I might as well enjoy it.

As Friend lapped at a pat of butter, Molly took a bite of oatmeal and said, "I don't suppose the fair will be open in this storm. . . ."

"No," I said. "No, I guess not."

Molly's forehead wrinkled. "Should we still take the money back today anyway?"

"I don't know," I said, remembering the crash of lamps. "It's raining pretty hard. But whatever you want to do is fine. I don't care. Either way."

Molly set down her spoon thoughtfully. "Is everything all right, Annie? You seem . . . different this morning."

"Yeah . . . I'm fine," I said.

"Are you, truly?"

"I *guess* I am."

"What's wrong? You can tell me."

"It's just . . . I thought I'd go home during the night," I confessed, shaking my head. "I'm not sure what it means that I didn't."

"Oh," she said. "Oh." Her mouth turned down slightly. "You mean, you don't *want* to stay?"

"It's not that," I said. "I *do* want to be here. Only . . . I don't like not knowing how to get back. And Mom—"

"I see," said Molly quietly. "Do you think perhaps I have to unwish you?"

"Oh!" I said. "I'm not sure. I hadn't thought about that."

"Do you want me to do that? I can try right now."

I nodded. "Would you? Try?"

Molly looked sad, but she closed her eyes, screwed up her face, and waved her hands above her head. "I wish," she said, "that Annie would go home right now!" She looked silly, like a little kid playing a game.

"Are you gone now?" she asked, opening one eye.

"Nope. Still here," I said.

Her face relaxed. "In that case," she said, "perhaps it *wasn't* my wish?"

"I guess not," I said. I forced a smile. "That must mean we have another day."

"We should make the most of it," said Molly.

"How do you want to do that?" I asked. "In this rain?"

"Well, you still haven't seen the hotel at all." Molly grinned.

When she said that, I remembered a shimmer. I

recalled a dusty lobby, a chandelier. Diamonds in the darkness. *Maybe*, I thought, *this is a good thing, this extra day*. "I'd like that," I said. "In fact, I'd like that a lot."

"The only problem," said Molly, "is that if we want to explore, we'll have to try going out to come in again." Her forehead wrinkled briefly. "Which means we *do* have to brave the storm. For a little while, at least."

"Maybe we should wait and see if the rain lets up," I suggested. "Give it a few hours?"

"Yes, that's a good idea," Molly said as she fed a sliver of bacon to the kitten. "That will give us some time with Friend before we go. We don't want him to think we've run away and deserted him."

Friend nuzzled her hand as though in agreement.

We finished our breakfast and our inevitable game of cards, then spent the morning playing with Friend in the bedroom, where we discovered that the kitten liked to chase everything. He pounced on Molly's slipper, and dragged the sleeping mask from under the bed, then chewed it until I rescued it and set it on the bedside table. Molly found this endlessly entertaining, but I got bored enough to read a *Look* magazine article about "How to See Europe on a Dollar a Day." A dollar a day!

When Nora arrived with lunch, we hurried back out to the sitting room, careful to close the bedroom door behind us. As we sat down at the table, I saw Friend's little claws scraping under the door. I didn't think Nora spotted him.

"Goodness, it's frightful out there today," said the maid, setting down her tray. "Cars are like to wash away. Count yourselves lucky you don't have to go out in that mess, girls." Molly kicked my leg under the table. I kicked her back.

After Nora was gone, we finished our sandwiches, which were made of something that looked like bologna but tasted better. Then Molly stood up. "Let's go see how awful it really is. Maybe Nora's exaggerating."

We tucked Friend safely away in the bedroom with a pile of pillows, some crumpled bits of paper to play with, and a dish of water. We raised the window in the bathroom and found that Nora was right. It was like a monsoon outside! The rain was coming down in a wall of water.

"What do you think?" Molly said. "It's very wet."

"That's how rain tends to be," I said. "But yeah, it's bad."

"I'll try if you will," said Molly. A gust of wind splattered rain right in our faces, but she put a hand on the sill and hoisted herself out. "It's not so bad," she called back in to me, sputtering water. "Once you get used to it."

"If you say so," I said as I pulled myself up beside her. "Here goes nothing." I crawled outside and a chilly wind took my breath away.

Molly was lying. There was no getting used to the storm. Rain pelted me like tiny needles, and the wind blew nonstop. I was soaked in seconds, and the railing and the stairs were terribly slick. I didn't even try to see what was happening with Molly. I focused on my own feet, gripped the railing tight, and held my breath. Step by step. Hand over hand.

When I slipped off the last step, the ground felt good under my feet, if squishy. "Whew!" I said, turning to Molly.

She was already dashing for cover, arms over her head. I raced behind her to a set of four steps that led down to a small door. Molly pulled it open and ducked inside. I followed her. The door closed behind me with a bang.

Inside the basement the air was warm and humid. A few bare bulbs hung from the ceiling of the dim, cavernous room. I followed Molly, dripping, through another door, into a laundry room where sheets were draped like ghosts from clotheslines. Molly put a finger to her lips. "Hush!"

There was an overpowering smell of bleach, dust, and damp, a rich scent that tickled my throat. Rainwater was dripping from my hair into my eyes. The warm basement felt good on my cold skin.

"I wish we had dry clothes," I whispered, trying to wring out my skirt.

Molly whirled around and grinned. "Oh! What a good thought." She made her way to one of the clotheslines. "Perfect," I heard her mutter. Then she was back with a pile of dark clothes and a rough towel. "Put these on."

I stripped off my wet clothes and dried off with the towel until I felt tingly. Soon I was dressed in a maid's uniform like Nora's. "The hat too?" I asked.

"The hat especially," said Molly, pulling hers on. "What a disguise! I bet we could walk right up to Papa and he wouldn't recognize us."

"I'm *sure* your dad would recognize you, Molly."

Molly only shrugged. "I'm just sorry there aren't any socks. These are squooshy."

"It *is* too bad," I agreed. "Mine are like dead fish."

"Ew." Molly wrinkled her nose. I wrinkled mine back at her, and we both grinned. It was much nicer in the warm, dry clothes, with the rubbed-clean feeling of a rain shower.

Then Molly picked up her wet things and jammed them deep down into a garbage can in a corner.

It felt weird to throw away perfectly good clothes. "Are you sure?" I said, looking back at her over my shoulder as I prepared to bury the wet clothes in the bin. "It's such a waste."

"I've plenty more," she said. "We don't want anyone to find them down here, do we?"

"I guess not." I crammed the wet things down with a broom handle.

By the time I turned around, Molly had walked over to the other end of the room. I watched as she climbed onto a pile of crumpled sheets and reached for a square hole in the brick wall. "Now, here we go," she said proudly.

"What is it?" I asked, peering up into the hole.

"It's a laundry chute," Molly said over her shoulder. "Haven't you been inside one before?"

"I've never even *seen* one."

"Really?" Molly looked surprised. "They're very good for getting around. Maggie and Ginny showed me how, a long time ago. I'll go first, and you can follow. All right?" Before I could answer, she climbed headfirst into the yawning mouth of the laundry chute and disappeared. I could just make out the soles of her shoes.

I stepped closer and looked up the chute. It was pitch-black in there. I reached out a hand and felt a slanted piece of metal. It was like Molly was climbing up a slide.

"Hey," I called up after her. "Where are we going, anyway?"

"Shhh," warned Molly from inside the chute. Then I heard only the faint squeak of her shoes and hands rubbing against metal. At last Molly's whisper echoed down tinnily, "I'm here! I made it! Now you!"

I climbed up into the dark square hole and made my way slowly. It was a little tight and I couldn't turn around. Briefly I thought about what would happen if I got stuck. But I kept climbing, even though the chute smelled like sweaty gym clothes and dirty pennies.

When I got to the top and peeked out, Molly wasn't there. I only saw more linens piled on the floor. Napkins, stained tablecloths, dishrags. In the next room I could hear a clatter.

"Molly?" I called softly.

"Who's there?" shouted back a man's voice.

"Oh!" I said without meaning to.

"Hello?" called the man again.

From above me in the chute I heard Molly's voice. "Hurry!" she urged.

"I'm trying," I whispered.

The second story took even longer because my arms and legs were tired and shaky from the strain of climbing. But this time when I stuck my head out, I found Molly smiling at me.

"Now jump!" she said.

· 10 ·

THE OPPOSITE OF CAKE

With tired arms, I pulled myself that last foot up the chute, then sat in the little door hole cut into the wall, my wet shoes dangling. I looked around. Tables and chairs were strewn about. One entire wall of the room was covered in plush green velvet curtains. The other walls were dark wood. The ceiling was high, which made the whole thing feel like a throne room in a castle.

"Come on." Molly beckoned below me.

I sprang down about three feet and landed on the purple carpet. My feet prickled.

Right away I could hear music, but it was smothered

by the chatter of people talking. There were thumps and scrapes, chairs being pushed in and out, and forks clattering against dishes. The music floated softly beneath these other, sharper noises.

"Oh, Molly!" I said, reaching out and squeezing her hand. This was nothing like the dusty hotel I'd seen back in my own time.

Molly beamed at me proudly, bouncing on her toes. "We're in the banquet hall," she said. "On the balcony above the ballroom. We never use this room when there's something happening below, because you can hear everything. Come on!"

I ran across the room after her and together we peeked through a slit in the heavy green curtains. The music swelled up at us. It was the song Molly had sung to Friend just the day before. "Can't take that away from me," we both sang softly.

"Jinx!" I said.

"What does *that* mean?" she asked. "What's *jinx*?"

"It's just this thing my friends and I do. If you say something at the exact same time as someone, you say 'jinx.' Then you get a wish. Or a Pepsi. Or a pizza. Except you never really get it."

Molly laughed. "That makes no sense at all. Also, what's a *peet-za*?"

I stared. *This* I could not believe. "You don't have pizza?"

Molly shook her head. "I don't think so. What is it?"

"Only the best food in the world. Food from heaven. Promise me that as soon as possible you'll eat a pizza."

"I promise," said Molly, nodding solemnly. "I do."

After that, the two of us turned our attention back to the scene below.

"Ooh," whispered Molly. "It's a wedding! Look."

I looked. Waiters were scurrying around with bottles and silver trays. There was smoke, so much smoke, drifting, rising from cigars and cigarettes up to the chandeliers. I swallowed a cough.

The men were nice-looking, with their suits and slicked-back hair, but the ladies were even better in their pale drapey dresses. Some had tiny furs hung around their necks. A few wore flowers, or had hats perched on their heads with feathers that shook when they danced. The bride, in white lace, was darting around, hugging everyone.

"I've never been to a wedding," I said. "It's so pretty!"

"Really?" Molly looked at me curiously. "There are loads of things I've never done, but I've been to weddings. What about your aunts and cousins? Surely they get married."

"I don't have any aunts or cousins," I said, shaking my head.

"I don't think I've ever heard of anyone not having cousins, except perhaps Little Orphan Annie."

"Plenty of people don't have cousins," I said. Though I couldn't actually think of any. "Hey, which one is your dad?"

Molly touched her maid's cap and shook the curls that peeped out from beneath. She scanned the crowd. "He never comes to events. He has things to do." But then she went rigid beside me and pulled the curtains closed with a *shush*.

"What?" I asked. "What is it?"

"I was wrong," she said. "He *is* there. Papa."

"Where?" I asked.

"It doesn't matter," she said, shaking her curls. "He was talking to a waiter, over in the corner. He didn't see me. Don't worry." But she sounded worried.

I put one careful eye back to the split between the curtains. At last I found the man with the mustache from Molly's picture.

"Does your dad have a yellow flower?" I whispered.

"Yes," she said without looking. "He always wears that, so everyone will know him."

"He doesn't *look* mean," I said, shaking my head. "He's smiling."

Molly shot me a funny look. "I never said he was mean. What gave you that idea?"

I shrugged. "Sorry. I don't know. Honestly, I don't know much about dads in general. They mow the lawn, right? And play golf? Or go bowling?"

Molly shook her head. "Not mine. He just works. Then he works some more. And more."

A few minutes later, the music faded and the crowd went silent. A large cake was wheeled into the room on a cart. The bride and groom came together to cut it, and my stomach growled. "There's the cake," I whispered. "I wish *we* had a piece—"

"Ooh! I know something!" shouted Molly suddenly. Her voice rang out above the now-quiet hall.

I froze.

Several people glanced up at the ceiling.

I ducked back behind the curtain.

Molly stood with her hand to her mouth. Her eyes went wide. "Do you suppose they heard that?" she hissed.

"Umm, I think it's highly possible," I said.

"Should we go? We *should* go, shouldn't we?"

"Probably," I said. "But why'd you *ooh*?"

"It was just—I had an idea. I wanted to—" Then she added, "Oh, fiddle! Let's try it anyway. We'll be quick, come on!" She dashed away from the curtains and back over to the wall, where she stood in front of a painting of an unsmiling woman holding a bouquet of flowers. I followed, then gasped when Molly gripped the picture frame and tugged at it. The frame swung out from the wall, revealing a hole. It was a dumbwaiter, like the one in *Harriet the Spy*!

"Cool! I wish *we* had one of those," I said.

"You don't? I feel sorry for your maids."

"Yeah, well, we don't have any of those either," I said.

"Cross your fingers," Molly said as she pulled on a thick rope inside the dumbwaiter.

"For what?" I said.

"Cake," said Molly. "Didn't you just make a wish?"

After a minute of pulling, a tiny platform arrived from below. Molly reached up to grab the tray in it, but when she lifted the silver dome, it was—*not* cake.

"Ugh," said Molly as she stared at the plate in her hand. "Bad timing. Liver and onions?"

I held my nose. The odor in the room was meaty and spoiled. "It smells like the *opposite* of cake," I said. "Send it back! Gross."

"Okay!" She reached up to set the plate in the dumbwaiter. That was when we heard footsteps, someone walking up the stairs.

I froze, but Molly moved fast. She set the plate down on the floor at her feet and hoisted herself up, first onto the table, and then into the dumbwaiter. "Hurry," she said, poking out her head. "Get in!"

"There's no room!" I said. I searched around for another place to go, but the laundry chute was over next to the doorway.

"I'll *make* room." She wiggled around.

The footsteps were close. Loud.

In a panic, I scrambled up onto the table, then tried to climb in with Molly. I crammed my body in beside her backward. "Oof!" I said, jamming my rear end in and sitting down. My legs still dangled below me.

"Come *on*," she said. "In. Now!" The footsteps were *there*.

I pulled my knees up to my chest, squished myself in, and wrapped my arms around my neck. "Now," I whispered. "Now!"

Molly pulled the heavy door, but it didn't quite close. She took a deep breath and gave one final tug, and it locked with a smooth click.

We were hidden now, but squashed like sardines in a can and pinching our noses against the vile smell of the liver. "What will happen if we get caught?" I whispered, catching a mouthful of her curls.

"They'll call Papa." Molly's voice trembled in my ear.

"What will *he* do?" I asked.

She didn't answer me. But I heard the wet sound of Molly chewing her nails. I shifted around, trying to get comfortable.

Then there were voices, men's voices.

"Mr. Moran thought he saw someone up here," said one voice. "Probably maids cheating off work. Or maybe it's nothing."

The other man snickered. "Well, *nothing* is more than enough reason for Moran to dock a maid's pay. The old skinflint."

I tried to pat Molly's shoulder. I thought it was her shoulder, anyway. The way we were crammed in, it could have been anything.

We listened to the two men move around. Then the first one said, "C'mon, there's nothing up here. I'm not wasting my time. Let's go have a smoke before we report back, hey?"

The other man grunted. "I like the sound of *that*."

I was about to heave a sigh of relief when there was a clatter and crash. "Now I've gone and done it!" shouted one of the men. "Would you look at this mess, gravy all over! Someone's been sneaking around up here after all."

The other man grumbled, "And now *we've* got to clean it. So much for that smoke. How's about you go and fetch a rag and bucket?"

"How's about *you*?" said the other. "I'll wait here."

"If *I'm* going, *you're* going." The two voices became fainter as the men headed away, stomping down the stairs.

Molly opened the door. We gasped for air and stared at each other. Then, at the exact same moment, we both whispered, "*That* was close!"

Molly paused, then whispered, "Ooh, ooh . . . *jinx*!" Then she said, "Like *that*? Did I do it right? The jinx?"

"Yeah," I said. "Totally. But now let's get to the chute and get gone."

Molly shook her head. "We can't use it now," she said. "The things they went to fetch are in the basement, just where the chute comes out. We'll be in the soup for sure if we slide down."

"In the soup?"

"In a pickle," said Molly.

"A pickle?"

"We'll get in *trouble*. Just stay put." She swung the

door shut again, and we were back in the stinky darkness. "Now grab the rope," she said. "We've got to go up."

I reached for the rope but got Molly's nose instead. "Ouch!" she said.

"Sorry."

"Shh," said Molly in a tiny hiss. "*Pull.*"

We pulled, hard as we could. Inch by inch. It took everything we had to move ourselves at all. I was sweating, and my palms were burning. I was wheezing, and so was Molly. "Did your sisters show you how to do this too?" I asked. "Like the laundry chute?"

"No," came Molly's voice. "They showed me how to sneak treats from it. But I guess I invented riding in it all by myself, just now."

"Oh," I said. "Well, if we do this again, let's bring a flashlight. It's too dark!"

"Just pretend you're wearing your sleeping mask," said Molly.

"But I don't actually *wear* that sleeping ma—" Then I cut myself off. "Oh," I said out loud, without meaning to. "Oh!"

"Annie! Shhh!" hissed Molly again.

"Sorry," I whispered. Only I couldn't stop thinking about it after that, the mask. *The mask!* Maybe *that* was why I was still here, still in the past. I'd come back in time wearing the mask. It only stood to reason that I'd need to be wearing the mask to go home again. The bed wasn't my wardrobe, my talisman. The *mask* was.

A sense of calm settled over me. It made so much sense! I smiled in the darkness. Nothing was quite so awful anymore. Except maybe the liver.

"Where are we going?" I asked as the dumbwaiter rose slowly through the hotel.

"I don't know," hissed Molly. "Not here."

We kept pulling.

"How do we know when to stop?" I asked.

Molly didn't answer me.

Up we went, in the smallest, slowest, darkest elevator in the universe. I kept thinking we'd see a door, but with no light, it was impossible to know when we were passing them. The rope groaned and stretched. The metal box scraped against the shaft, but we just kept going blindly. I tried as hard as I could not to think about the rope breaking. I tried not to think about the shaft below us, and how much heavier we were together than a plate of liver and onions. Finally we came to a place where no matter how I pulled, we didn't move. We were either stuck or done.

"Molly?" I said. "What do we do now?"

"I suppose we push," said Molly.

So we pushed. At first nothing happened. Then something came loose, and the door made a clicking sound and swung open to reveal, amazingly, Molly's own canopy bed.

"No way!" I shouted. "How lucky is *that*?"

"Like magic," said Molly, letting herself down onto the rug.

I followed, hanging on to the dumbwaiter door, which turned out to be the painting of the chubby dog, set on a hinge in the wall.

"And it was there all this time?" said Molly, shaking her head up at me in disbelief.

"All this time," echoed a voice.

· 11 ·

LIST OF GOOD IDEAS

I turned my head so fast my braid whipped me in the face.

Standing in the doorway, staring at us, was Nora.

Before I had a chance to say a word, Molly's back went rigid. Her chin lifted. Mistress Mary opened her mouth to speak, but then—

She saw the kitten, and her anger melted. Her face softened. Friend was curled happily in Nora's hand, nibbling some tidbit. Molly looked at the ball of fur.

"Oh," Molly said. "You're taking care of Friend."

She stroked the cat's tiny head. "He's a sweet little man," she said.

"I found him," Molly said. "In a garbage pail."

Nora paused. Then she gave a pert nod and said, "Lucky for both of you, I'd say. Every child deserves a pet, and every pet deserves a child."

"I can explain," said Molly.

Nora shook her head. She handed over Friend. "Isn't my business, miss."

"But aren't you supposed to report things like this to Papa?" Molly asked.

Nora sighed. "Maybe I am, but I won't. I just won't. It isn't right. No child should be so alone. From now on I'll be minding my own business, I think."

"Really?"

"All I ask is that you be careful. Can you do that?"

Molly nodded, still looking stunned.

Nora turned to me. "As for *you*, I don't know who you are, or quite what you're doing here. But I'll trust that you mean well, and that you won't put Miss Molly in danger. That you'll help her."

"I'll do my best," I said.

"Lastly," said Nora as she turned to leave, "I left some newspapers in the bathroom for you. They might come in handy for your little man. I don't want to be cleaning up any more messes like the one I found in the closet just now, hey? Put those maid uniforms to good use."

"Oops," said Molly.

Nora nodded. "Oops is right."

After dinner, Molly and I played a game of chess. Or we started to, until it became clear I would never, ever win a game. "Molly?" I said, giving up and lying down on the floor. "I wonder, if you could do anything tomorrow, absolutely anything, what would you do?"

"Well," said Molly, "I suppose to begin with I'd go back to that store, to pay for the lamps. So I could stop feeling so guilty."

"Okay," I said. "But besides *that*, where would you go? For fun?"

"I know!" said Molly. "Let's make a list. Of all the places we mean to go, all the things we want to do. First thing, Woolworth's! Second, I want to go to that fair, with the Ferris wheel."

"Sure," I said. "But also, I want to see the water. Put that on the list too."

Molly got up and found a box of stationery and a nubby pencil. Underneath the words FROM THE DESK OF MARY MORAN and a spray of lilacs, Molly wrote:

List of good ideas to do sooner or later, but hopefully sooner

1. Pay for the lamps.
2. Go to the fair.
3. Learn to roller-skate.
4. Visit the water.

"*Then* what?" she asked.

"I want to go to Egypt," I said. "To see the pyramids! Don't you?"

"Well, yes," she said, "that would be marvelous. But we probably can't do that tomorrow."

"Probably not," I admitted. "But I didn't think I'd get to see 1937 either, so let's write *everything* down. Who knows what crazy thing might happen!"

"In that case," she said, "I'd like to fly."

"How are you planning to manage that?"

She shrugged. "I don't know, but three days ago, it seemed impossible I'd ever see the backyard again, so if you get Egypt, I get flying. Make sense?"

"Sure." I laughed. "Why not? We're dreaming, after all. In which case, I want to be rich someday, super rich. Write that one down."

Molly scribbled, then looked up. "I want to get married and have a family. And I want to do good things too.

I want to help people. But I don't know how just yet. Maybe I'll be a nurse." She scribbled something down. "Also, I want to meet Fred Astaire."

"Write down about the pizza," I said. "That's P-I-Z-Z-A."

"Oh, I almost forgot," she said.

"And I want to be in a movie," I said. "And I want to stop biting my nails."

"And I want," said Molly, "to save someone's life. . . ."

"Wow," I said, sitting up. "That's a big one."

"Yes, it is," said Molly, looking down at her list. "Perhaps that's enough for now. Perhaps it's time to go to bed. We can think of more things to add tomorrow, can't we? We can just keep adding to the list forever."

That night, as we lay in bed with Friend curled between us, Molly drifted into her drugged sleep. I watched her and listened to the kitten purr. When at last I reached down to tug the sleeping mask from under the mattress, I found I was sad. Now I didn't *want* to leave again. I wanted to do the list of things with Molly. Funny, when I thought I was stuck, I felt desperate to go home; but now that I'd figured out my return, I wished I could stay.

I thought about *The Lion, the Witch and the Wardrobe* kids, those Pevensies. Had they felt this way, when they became queens and kings in Narnia? Had they missed their mom and dad? I didn't remember the books talking about that.

Of course I would leave. I had a life of my own to live, and Mom. Still, the idea of trading in this Molly for that old lady Molly—ugh.

I looked over at Molly and wished there was some way to say goodbye. Then I had a thought. I *could* say goodbye. I could leave something, some shred of me, for Molly to find once I was gone. I climbed out of bed and looked around for the box of stationery. I didn't see it, but my eyes fell on her copy of *The Secret Garden*. So I took up Molly's fountain pen and turned to the last page, to the very back of the book. There I wrote:

Dear Molly,

By the time you read this, I'll be gone. I hope you'll understand that I needed to go home to my mom.

I know you'll be sad, but I want you to know that I'll miss you. A lot. I've never had a friend like you before.

Give Friend a kiss for me, and say goodbye to Nora.

And someday, I promise, you'll see me again. Someday I'll come back to the hotel, and you'll look up, and I'll be there. It might be a long time, but I swear it! I do.

LYLAS! (that means Love Ya Like A Sister)

Your friend,

Annie

PS: Have fun at the fair!

Feeling better, I got back into bed, pulled the covers up, and reached for the sleeping mask. I fingered the jet beads and the smooth fabric, then noticed something. The elastic wasn't stretched out anymore, and the beads weren't coming loose. The mask looked like new. How had *that* happened? Was the mask repairing itself? Was there more magic at work? What did the transformation mean?

I was calm as I pulled it over my head, ready. "I'll see you soon, Mom," I whispered into the quiet room as I settled the mask on my eyes.

Then everything went dark . . .

But not dark enough. Not quite.

There was no static, no beat, no strange silence.

I was still in the past. Molly was breathing heavily beside me and Friend was snuffling in his sleep. I hadn't disappeared. I lay in the bed, still wearing the mask, and

I couldn't see anything and I couldn't think what to do next. Did this mean I couldn't go home? I didn't understand what was going on. It felt very wrong.

I swallowed hard. Now what?

It was 1937. It was still 1937.

How would I get home? Would I *ever* get home?

I ripped off the mask and looked around the room but found nothing to help me. Beside me, Molly stirred, shifting onto her side. Still there, breathing over my thoughts. I tried to ignore her. It wasn't time to think about Molly. It was time to think about *me*, about *Mom*.

I took a deep breath and tried again to backtrack, to remember all the details. What was I still missing?

Maybe I had to actually sleep in the mask. Maybe that was it! Mom would say it does no good to freak out. "When one thing doesn't work," she always said, "chill out and try something else."

It was the only thing I could think to do. I could try again. I could keep trying. I could sleep. In and out, deep and slow, in and out, push and pull, calming me, settling me. Slower and slower. Deeper and deeper. Each heavy breath like a wave lapping at the shore. In and out, in and out. Each breath calm and regular.

Sleep would come. It had to.

· 12 ·

DRAGGING A FISH

A banging woke me. A thumping, knocking sound. Then a voice. "Hello?" the voice called. "Hello? Miss Moran?"

Miss Moran?

I rolled over, tangled in sheets and dreams. The fog seeped back in, and I drifted backward, into sleep.

"Miss Moran! Molly! Are you decent?"

I opened my eyes again, sat up, and tugged off the sleeping mask. Instantly I was swamped with a wave of dizziness. The room swirled and I fell back. "Molly?" I mouthed as the ceiling swam. I knew that name, even in my fog. "Molly."

"Shhh!" Beside me, a girl was awake, a tiny kitten curled in her hair.

I stared at her. She had a finger to her lips.

Inside my head everything was still blurry and shifting. But I knew her. Molly? I closed my eyes and memories washed over me. My face streaming with rain, a cramped dark place. But who was at the door now? What came next?

Molly sat up, and the kitten rolled away from her and stretched. "Dr. Irwin!" she choked.

I whispered, "Who? What should I—"

She pointed below the bed. "There," she whispered. She shoved the kitten at me, and I took it. I stared at her, baffled. I still didn't know anything! So much I couldn't remember. What was happening now?

Molly called toward the door, "Yes, Dr. Irwin, just—one second, please. Let me—ahem, finish with these buttons!" Molly gestured wildly. She pointed beneath the bed again. "Go, Annie," she said softly, and I went.

As Molly reached for a dressing gown and pulled it on, I half fell over the side, onto the floor with a thump. Still foggy, now bruised.

"One more minute," called Molly, eyeing me on the floor. "I'm nearly ready."

I scrambled beneath the bed, the kitten tucked beneath my arm.

"Come in!" Molly shouted.

I heard the door open and saw the bottom of it swing wide. Two brown shoes approached. I felt the creaking of wood and springs above me as the doctor—not a small man, I guessed—sat down with a groan.

I squeezed my eyes and crossed my fingers. There was no question about what would happen to me if the bed collapsed. The kitten curled up against my neck and began to purr. It sounded like a motorcycle in the distance. I could feel the rumble in my jawbone. I only hoped nobody could hear it on the bed above. My nose tickled. I knew that I should not sneeze.

"It took you so long to answer the door," boomed the voice above me, startling me from my thoughts. "I began to think that maybe you weren't in. Har. Har." The doctor had one of those unfunny joking voices grown-ups sometimes use.

"Oh," said Molly with a nervous giggle. "I'm always here. I just sleep very deeply. Because of . . . my medicine. Where else would I be?"

The doctor ignored her question. "Now, say *ahhhh!*"

Molly opened her mouth. "*Ahhhh!*"

While Molly breathed and coughed and answered questions, I lay beneath the massive bed and tried to piece things together. I backtracked through the day before and the day before that. The laundry chute, the ballroom, and the liver. Nora's smile.

I pushed past that, to an old lady in a bed. I felt a dazzle of memory there, a spark, and then a flame caught—and I remembered! I was Annie Jaffin, and my mother was Ruby Jaffin, and she was back there, in the memory, in—the future? While I was huddled in the dusty underneath of the past.

I lay among the dust bunnies, pulling the memory out of the murk, like I was dragging a fish slowly from a river. I tried to keep the line steady. I didn't want to lose what I'd caught. In a rush, my life came tumbling back to me—*Cosby Show* Susie Ice Capades science fair project. Home.

How had I lost all of that? How had I forgotten? And how could I keep it from slipping again? The mask hadn't worked. Maybe nothing would. I closed my eyes and buried my face in the warm purring side of the tiny kitten.

I heard a shuffling sound and looked over at the door, where I could see Nora's black chunky heels and the hem of her dark skirt.

"Well, you're still on the mend!" the doctor said cheerily at last. "Though I must say, you are a little more constricted than last time. I suppose it could be dust, or smoke from outside."

"I'll close the window," offered Molly.

"Yes, do. And please don't overexert yourself. I know it can be hard for a girl your age to sit still, but don't let your improving health fool you. This is still serious."

"I understand," said Molly in a docile tone.

"You must take care of yourself as you begin to feel better," the doctor said. "You could have an attack at any time." Then he called out, as if to someone standing in the next room, "Looks good, James! She's doing fine."

James? I saw there was a new pair of shoes in the doorway beside Nora's: men's shoes, black and shiny.

Molly, in a mixture of startled confusion and childish delight, burst out, "Papa!" just as the kitten scratched me good on the neck. My eyes watered as I grabbed his face to keep him still. I had to bite my lip to keep from yelping, but even so, a breath escaped too loudly.

There was silence above me.

I froze, still holding the kitten's jaws. His tail twitched. His claws dug into my hand.

Molly spoke again, her tone eager. "Papa? I'm glad to see you. It's been so long since—"

A stern voice interrupted her. "Yes. Hello there, Mary. Things are busy downstairs. How are you today?"

"I'm better, Papa!" Molly's voice was painfully cheery.

"I'm pleased to hear that," said her father. "I'll be sure to tell your mother when I speak to her." The shiny black shoes stayed at the door. Then, after a beat of silence, they turned and walked away. The stern voice called out, "I must get back to work now. Be well, Mary."

The delight was gone when Molly said, "Oh! All right, Papa. See you soon. . . ."

"Now you get better right away, you hear me?" said the doctor, snapping something shut—a bag, I supposed—with a final click. "That's an order. Har har. And don't eat too much pudding. I know how you children are, with your pudding."

Molly didn't say anything.

I heard the man groan once more as he stood, and the mattress gave a sigh of relief. I waited as the feet shuffled out; I waited to hear the door close in the sitting room. Even after that, I waited, with Friend squirming in my arms.

"Feh!" I said, spitting out dust. Once I was standing, I wiped my face and hair clean. "I think I need a bath." I dropped Friend on the bed.

"I was worried," said Molly quietly. "If Papa had seen—"

"You were lucky, miss," said Nora, stepping back into the room.

Molly whispered grimly, "Lucky. Yes, I'm so very lucky. What with all my pudding and everything."

Nora patted Molly's shoulder. "Come now, girls, get yourselves dressed. Breakfast is ready. Pancakes!"

Friend let out a mew, as though he knew what "pancakes" meant, and Nora turned. "I've a few sardines for you too, you scampy scrap."

"So," I said, reaching for syrup, "that was your dad."

Molly ignored me and began to spoon up grapefruit in tiny bites.

"Shall we look at our list?" I asked, chewing. "Pick something to do today?"

Molly nodded.

"Or should we stay in? The doctor did say you need to take it easy."

Molly frowned. "He always says that." Then she shouted out, "Oh, Nora!"

"Yes, miss?" Nora was heading for the door with last night's dishes.

"How much do you suppose something like a pretty glass lamp shade might cost? At the Woolworth's store. Just out of curiosity."

"Hmm. I'd wager about six dollars, if I had to guess," she called over her shoulder. "Why do you ask?"

"No reason," said Molly.

"No reason, eh?" Nora shot her a funny look as she closed the door behind her.

I did the math. There had to have been at least six lamp shades. In a world where a Hershey bar cost a penny, there was no way Molly had forty dollars lying around.

But after breakfast was over, Molly reached into a box on her bookshelf and came out with a thick roll of bills.

"Whoa! Where did you get *that*?" I exclaimed. Even in 1987, it would have been a lot of money for a kid to have. I'd never had forty dollars, I didn't think.

Molly shrugged. "We get pocket money, Ginny and Maggie and me. I've never had a chance to spend mine. But Papa's very fair, so he pays me each Sunday, just like the others. I've been saving for a long time. Years." She shoved the money deep into her pocket.

Outside, the rain was gone, but it had brought cool air. Below me trees swayed. The wind was strong as I leaned into the railing. In the street an engine sputtered to life. A man in a hat was getting into a car.

"Hey," I said, elbowing Molly, "isn't that your dad again?"

Molly nodded.

For a minute we were both quiet. Then Molly said, "Annie?"

"Uh-huh?" I looked at her.

"You really want to go home, don't you? To your mother?"

"Sure," I said. "Of course. And I will. It'll work out. It has to."

"But you never mention your father at all," Molly added. "Why is that?"

"Because I don't have a father," I said. "It's only me and Mom."

"I'm sorry," said Molly right away. "I didn't know."

"It's fine," I said. "Really, no big deal. He left us. I never knew him."

"Maybe that's just as well," said Molly, staring out at the street.

"Well, yeah, but only because my mom is super cool," I said.

Molly looked puzzled. "I don't understand."

"Hmm. It's kinda like—" I tried to think of a way to explain. "Life *might* be better if you had four hands, right?"

"What?" Molly was smiling now. "No! You'd look *very* queer."

"Well, yeah, but you could hold a book and eat spaghetti at the same time! You could do things twice as fast. The thing is, two hands are plenty, and that's what you're used to. So you've never thought to want four."

"I . . . suppose."

"My mom is like that. She's two hands. She's plenty. And she was, long before I knew I was supposed to have a dad. So I never thought to want one."

"*Plenty* sounds nice," said Molly. "What sort of person is she, your mom?"

I didn't know what to say. Mom was just Mom.

"Annie?"

"Mom's just—she's my *person*, I guess," I said. My voice felt shaky. I didn't like it. "She makes terrible jokes and always runs late. But she's—*there*. You know? She heats up soup when I'm sick. She reads to me, even though I can read to myself. She yells, and I yell back, and that's okay. She isn't perfect, but she's *mine*. Does that make sense?"

Molly was looking at me intently. Her eyes were focused, constant. "Would you like to know something?" she asked.

"Sure," I said.

Molly took a deep breath. "I would jump from this fire escape right now to feel that way about someone."

For a minute we stared at each other. It was weird. I didn't know how to respond. At last I said, "Is that true? Really?"

Molly shrugged. "Probably not, no. But it *feels* true."

"Well, that sucks," I said. "But jeez, stop being such a drama queen! You scared me." I punched her lightly in the arm.

Molly smiled faintly. "I don't know what a *drama queen* is," she said. "But I'll try not to be one. All right?"

"Anyway," I said, "of course your mother loves you too. And you love her. Right?"

Molly leaned over the railing. She looked a little sheepish. "Yes, I do," she said. "Certainly I do. But she isn't here, is she?"

"So you miss her! And you're mad. Like I said, my mom's not perfect either. Once she forgot to pick me up from ballet class and I had to walk home two miles in the dark! I wanted to kill her. Totally normal."

"Totally normal?"

"Totally."

Molly looked strangely relieved. "That's nice to know," she said.

· 13 ·

INSTEAD OF A HOME

After all that talking, it felt good to run down the fire escape with the wind in my face and the thud of my feet on the stairs. I kept a hand lightly on the railing, but I took each floor fast, whipping around corners. It felt like flying.

At the bottom I shot straight out into the alley, Molly behind me. She was smiling again. Soon we were at the fair poster, staring at its bright colors.

"Fell's Point," I read from the poster. "Is that far?"

"I don't know," said Molly. "But a taxi driver is sure

to. Look," she added, pointing to the list of attractions. "There's a fortune teller!"

"And a mermaid," I said, scanning the list. "*That* can't be real."

"*Probably* not," said Molly.

We headed down the alley to the big avenue, where we'd seen taxis two days before. But when we spotted a policeman blocking the sidewalk, we nodded at each other slowly and turned right at the intersection instead of left, *away* from the Woolworth's, as fast as we could hustle.

"We'll go back with the money when he's not there," she said. "After the fair. All right?"

"Sounds good to me!"

After a few blocks, we passed a large square brick building with a paved courtyard. Sitting around it were lots of girls wearing simple brown dresses. A few of them played jacks. Mostly they talked quietly in small groups. "Must be recess," I said.

Off to one side, two girls about my age were doing a hand clap, quickly but in hushed voices. One wore her hair in tight dark braids, the other in a mousy bob. I tried to listen but couldn't make out the song, so I walked into the yard with Molly a step behind me. When the clappers saw us, they stopped clapping.

"No, don't stop!" I said. "Keep singing. Please?"

They began again, slowly at first, then picking up speed. The one with the bob sang:

I am a pretty little Dutch girl,
As pretty as I can be, be, be,
And all the boys in the neighborhood
Are crazy over me, me, me.
My boyfriend's name is Fatty,
He comes from Cincinnati,
With turned-up toes and a pimple on his nose,
And this is how the story goes.

Molly burst into cheerful laughter when they were done. "How terrific!" she said. "Where did you learn to do that?"

"I don't know," said the girl with the bob. "Who doesn't know how to clap?"

"I don't," said Molly.

I hadn't done a hand clap in about a year myself. There was an unwritten law of the schoolyard that girls graduated from hand claps to cheers when they started fifth grade. I'd moved on from "Eenie Meanie Bopsabeanie" to "Be Aggressive." But now my hands itched with wanting to join in. I rubbed them on my skirt.

That was when the girl with the braids looked up at me and held out her hands in a questioning way. "You vant?" she asked. She had a strong accent and a shy smile.

"Sure," I said quickly. "Thanks!" I sat down on the grass opposite her as the girl with the bob stood up. "You want to do that one again, or do you maybe want to learn a new song?" I asked.

The girl smiled eagerly, and as we began to clap, I sang:

Miss Lucy had a steamboat,
The steamboat had a bell.
Miss Lucy went to heaven,
and the steamboat went to
HELLO, operator,

When I got to that line, a small group of girls tittered behind me. I glanced back and realized we were attracting a crowd. Molly was beaming. I sang:

Please give me number nine.
And if you disconnect me,
I will chop off your . . .

More girls had joined us. This time, when I got to the punch line, the girls behind me chorused the obvious.

BEHIND the 'frigerator,
There was a piece of glass.
Miss Lucy sat upon it
And cut her big fat . . .

I was caught up in it now, having such a good time, singing and clapping. I kept going.

ASK me no more questions,
I'll tell you no more lies.
The boys are in the bathroom,
Zipping up their . . .

Now the girl opposite me was blushing, but she was also still clapping, so I sang on, a little faster.

FLIES are in the meadow,
The bees are in the park.
Miss Lucy and her boyfriend
Are kissing in the . . .

DARK is like a movie,
A movie's like a show,
A show is like a TV set
And that is all I know!

I finished, breathless. The girl with the braids grinned and Molly burst out laughing. The other girls around us broke into light applause. In the grass a few feet away, another pair was already attempting a slightly messy version of "Miss Lucy." When they got to the words *TV set*, they said it like one big word: "TEEVEESET!" The way I sang the songs I learned in French class: "FRAYERAJOCKAFRAYERAJOCKADORMAYVOODORMAYVOO." Memorized sounds, not words. "TEEVEESET!"

I chuckled.

"Vat is funny?" asked the girl opposite me.

"Oh, nothing," I said. "Thanks, that was really fun. Do you want to do another, or will recess be over soon? It's funny you have school in the summer."

"School?" The girl looked puzzled.

"No, Annie, look," said Molly, pointing to a plaque on the building. "This *isn't* a school."

I looked up. "The Baltimore Home for Girls," I read out loud.

"Excepting it's not a *home*, not really," called out a voice. A girl a little older than the rest was standing off to one side. She had blond hair and pale blue eyes. She stared at me, hands on hips. "It's *instead* of a home. Which isn't the same at all. Who're you?"

"I'm Annie," I said. "Who're you?"

"Geneva." She didn't add anything, and she didn't take her eyes off me.

"Wait, so is this an—" I almost couldn't bring myself to say it.

"Orphanage?" Geneva spat the word out. "Sure is."

"An orphanage," echoed Molly beside me.

"That so hard to believe?" asked Geneva.

Molly said, "I just always thought there would be a fence at an orphanage. Like in Dickens. Also—you don't look hungry."

I stared at Molly. I couldn't believe she'd said that, but I had to admit, it was sort of what I'd been thinking too. These girls looked fine to me. Clean clothes, and they seemed happy, with their jacks and their hand claps. Not the way I'd pictured orphans at all.

Geneva shrugged. "Why would they need a fence? They'd be happy if I left. They'd give my spot to the next girl, and I'd be sorry. My folks brought me here for a reason, you know?"

I was confused. "Folks? You mean, you have parents?"

"Not *much* parents," snorted Geneva. "But Pa would thrash me if I ran off. I'm not hungry *because* I'm here."

"I don't understand." Molly's eyes were wide. "Your parents *brought* you here? So you aren't actually an orphan?"

Geneva shrugged. "There were eight of us, a couple too many. Belle has a mom and pop too, right, *Belle*?" She sneered faintly at the girl with the braids sitting in front of me so quietly.

The girl sighed. "My name . . . it is *Bayla*, not *Belle*." She said this gently but firmly. I didn't think she liked Geneva very much. I didn't think I did either.

Geneva tossed her head, as if to say "*Whatever*." She stalked off.

"Bayla?" I said, turning back to my new friend. "Am I saying it right?"

She nodded happily. "Is correct."

"It's a pretty name," said Molly. "I've never heard it before. *Bayla*."

"It vas my grandmother's."

"That's nice," I said.

"Yes," said Bayla. She paused a moment, then motioned after Geneva. "It is true, vat she says. My parents, dey are alive, I *tink*."

"You *think?*" Molly asked. "How can you not know?"

Bayla shrugged. "I've not heard from home in two years. Dey sent me to America, to be safe. Only my aunt dat I am living wit, she dies of a fever." Bayla's dark eyes were huge. "But I am *not* an orphan. Dey vill come. I know."

"You came here to be safe?" I asked. "Safe from what?"

She shook her head. "My country. Is bad now. Very bad."

I wanted to say the right thing, but I had no idea what that might be, or what she meant, really. "I'm sorry," I offered.

"Is not your fault," said Bayla. She waved goodbye and turned toward the building. All the girls seemed to be filing inside now.

Molly and I headed slowly back to the street, then walked a few blocks in silence.

"It's incredible," Molly said at last. "That they can laugh and play like that. That they can be happy, even though . . ." Her voice trailed off.

"I wonder," I said, "what was so bad that Bayla's parents had to send her away."

"On the radio they say a war is coming," said Molly. "In Europe."

Dim pictures flashed through my mind, muddy gray images of men in uniforms, fighting in trenches. Tanks rolling through towns. "Oh," I said. "Yeah. It must be World War Two, huh? That's awful. I can't even imagine."

"World War Two?" Molly stopped walking.

"Yeah, didn't you already have World War One?"

"I don't know what that means. Do you mean the Great War?"

"I—I'm not sure." I didn't remember much from our world history unit, and anyway, it didn't seem like something Molly wanted to know about the future. "Either way, it's sad for Bayla." I started walking again, away from the conversation.

After another minute Molly cleared her throat. "Annie, I've been thinking . . . do you remember how you asked what would happen if Papa caught us?"

"Uh-huh," I said.

"Well, I think *that* might be what would happen. That place."

"You're nuts," I said. "He'd never turn you out. Why do you say things like that? Yeesh. Drama queen."

"Oh, not to me," Molly said, looking flustered. "To—you."

"Me?" I stopped walking. "But . . . *I'm* not an orphan."

"I know you have a mother, but she isn't here now. And those other girls weren't really orphans either, not the way I think of orphans."

"Ugh," I said. "Can we please not talk about this anymore?"

"All right," said Molly. Then she suddenly jerked her head up, shouted "Hey, hey!" and started waving both hands in the air like a maniac. Moments later a big car, black and boxy, pulled up. The sign on top read TAXI.

Molly stepped up onto the running board beneath the passenger side door and looked into the open window. The driver leaned over and stretched an arm across the seat. "Out on your own this sunny morning? Just the two of yous?"

"Yes," said Molly. "It *is* sunny, isn't it? The wind is dying down."

The driver nodded. "Well, then, climb on in. An' where'll you be heading?"

"To Fell's Point," said Molly, opening the door.

"Fell's Point?" The driver looked surprised.

"There's a fair," said Molly. "We think."

"Ahh." He relaxed. "Sure is, an' I'd be pleased to give yous a ride." He began to whistle. "It's just not a place I generally take young ladies."

Molly held up some paper money. "Is this enough?" she asked. The driver's eyes grew wide. "By all means," he said. "Welcome, welcome!"

Molly climbed in and I followed her, settling on the

wide seat, still thinking about the home that wasn't a home but trying not to. Idly, I ran my finger along the silky black fringe beneath the window. I'd been in taxis a few times, but I'd never seen one like this.

"Neither of us has ever been to Fell's Point," chattered Molly. "Is it nice? Is it near the water?"

The driver turned around. "You can't get much nearer the water," he said. "But *nice* isn't quite the word I'd choose. Rough types down by the docks."

"Oh," said Molly, sounding worried.

The driver looked back and laughed. "Don't worry. When the fair comes to town, it's different. It's grand!"

In a heartbeat we were speeding along, bumping down the road. There were no seat belts in the car, so Molly and I jounced as we zoomed along a brick street lined with stately homes. I couldn't ponder anymore, not bouncing and jumping and jerking like that. I couldn't help laughing. We passed a small park, where some little boys were throwing rocks into a fountain. I craned my neck to see the building above them, a tall white tower with a statue at the top. "What's that?" I asked.

"Why, *that* is the Washington Monument!" the driver proclaimed.

Then I had a thought. "Sir," I said, "you seem to know a lot about the city."

"I'm sort of an expert, it's true," he said. "And you can call me Frank."

"I wonder, Frank, do you know why sometimes it smells like cinnamon?"

"Ahh," Frank said. "That's the spice factory, down along the water. Some days the whole city smells like the perfume of the Orient, don't it?"

"I guess," I said. "That or an oatmeal cookie."

Frank laughed. "Fair enough."

Molly winked at me. "Is it the oldest spice factory in America, by any chance?"

"Well, as a matter of fact, I think it is," said Frank. "Oldest in the nation, tallest too. George Washington slept there hisself, as a matter of fact. Mighty famous, it is."

"Oooh. And what's that?" asked Molly as we turned, pointing to a huge gleaming square building with white columns and a grand archway.

"Our new library," said the man proudly. "Just rebuilt it! My cousin worked on the job. Don't it have more books than any library in the world? Or my name ain't Frank Callahan! Over there's the cathedral, oldest one in the country!"

"Hmm," I said.

"That's *quite* impressive," said Molly.

After that we stared out the window at the world speeding by. Whether or not everything was in fact the biggest and the oldest and the best like Frank seemed to think, there *was* a lot to see. All around were beautiful churches and statues. Then we turned down another street and rumbled through a neighborhood with smaller buildings, littler houses. There were more people on the streets here. We passed tiny storefronts and what looked like warehouses. In one place, a long line of people snaked around a corner.

"Why do you think they're standing in line?" I asked Molly. "What are they waiting for?"

"I don't know," said Molly.

Frank heard us and looked over his shoulder with surprise. "They're waiting for bread, of course," he said.

"Bread? Is it *that* good, the bread?" asked Molly.

"It's free," said Frank. "That's the best bread of all, for some folks."

"Oh," said Molly, sitting back. Her hand crept over her bulging pocket.

From part of yet another history lesson, a picture surfaced in my mind of men in a line, with hats pulled low over their faces, coats tight against the cold. *The Great Depression*, I thought to myself. The Great Depression was happening in 1937. Locked in the hotel, full of creamed chicken, I hadn't even considered what was happening outside. Funny how being shut away could make you forget everything else, like being sick for a week and coming back to school. While everyone who could afford to be in the hotel was dancing and drinking and wearing fine clothes, life outside was . . . different. I was only now getting to see it.

Molly hung over the front seat. "But *why* are those people so poor?" she asked. "Why don't they get jobs?"

"Well, surely you know it's been hard times for many." The driver looked bewildered by Molly's question. "Hard to find work."

Molly stammered. "I—I've been ill. I don't go out often. Until just recently."

"But you're better now?" asked the driver. "You look fit as a fiddle to me."

"Yes," said Molly thoughtfully. "Yes, I think I *am* much better."

Then the taxi was pulling up to a curb. Quick as a wink, Frank was out of his seat and dashing around to open our door, as though we were royalty. I climbed out as Molly paid him.

"I'd get you closer if I could, but this time of day the market stalls block the road," said Frank.

"That's all right," said Molly. "We don't mind walking!"

"Hey, girls, I'll tell you what," Frank called out as we walked away. "I'll be back here in this very spot in two hours' time, or as close to that as I can make it. In case ya need me. Watch the clock." He pointed to a church tower a few blocks away. "I don't like the idea of yous girls having no way to get back uptown."

"Thank you," said Molly brightly, turning and smiling. "That's kind of you."

Frank looked at the money in his hand. "Sure. I'm a kind feller."

We watched his car disappear, and then we turned around, toward the water. What a sight it was! Down at the end of the street was the harbor, full of men unloading boats onto an old pier. Seagulls soared and screeched. Off in the distance we could just make out the noise and color of the fair, and the Ferris wheel rising above a row of houses.

But between us and the fair was something else—a building a block long, surrounded by stalls and carts and horses and stands. Two stories tall, with great glass windows, it was swarmed on all sides by people selling things. BROADWAY MARKET, read the sign above the great doors.

There were fish and fruit and flowers. One man was

hammering at the sole of a shoe while his customer stood waiting on one leg. I saw a dentist pulling a man's tooth, while right beside him a woman was buying bananas. There were butchers hacking pieces off of animals right there in the street. I watched as one of them swept the extra bits—the ears and tails—into a basket. At the stall beside him, a woman was wringing a chicken's neck.

"It's like—" said Molly. "It's like this is where *everything* comes from."

But there was something else that struck me about the place, something I couldn't figure out at first. Something that reminded me of home. At last it hit me. In the hotel, and on all the streets we'd driven past, all the blocks we'd walked, everyone had been *white*. White everywhere.

Here the world was teeming with people speaking different languages, in all kinds of clothes. It was like the breadline. The farther we got from the hotel, the bigger the world felt, and the more I remembered.

Molly was staring every which way to take it all in. "I never *thought*," she said. "I never knew there was so much out here, *all* of this." Her eyes were shining. She was smiling. "Oh, Annie—it's like from a story. But bigger than a story. It's been here all this time. I never knew."

· 14 ·

THE MERMAID AND THE ALLIGATOR MAN

As we headed away from the market, toward the fair, the smells and the sounds began to change. Music drowned the market noise, and the odor of fish was replaced with the scent of popping corn and burnt sugar. My steps grew quicker. We sped through the rows of houses. Then I noticed something. "Look at those!" I said, pointing.

We were passing tiny houses now, with low roofs. They looked ancient, made of dark cracked bricks. Some of the houses had hitching posts, and some had window boxes full of flowers. But the doors were the best. They had colorful pictures painted right onto their screens, landscapes of villages, dotted with red-roofed villas and trees. I stopped and ran my fingers along a screen.

"Why do you think they paint them? They can't see the picture from inside."

"No," said Molly. "But when they're coming home at the end of the day, they can. It's like they're walking into someplace else. I think it's nice!"

I did too, but just then we turned a corner and arrived under the Ferris wheel. Here was the fair! Off in the distance, on the grandstand, a band was playing waltzy happy music. Up and down the brick streets all around us were brightly striped tents covered with big posters that advertised amazing sights, stupendous acts, and otherworldly creatures, painted in such bright colors it was hard to imagine any of it was real. All except the bearded lady, who didn't look all *that* amazing to me. We had one of those working at our grocery store in Atlanta. Best of all was a picture of two beautiful Siamese sisters with long golden curls, connected at the back.

Molly stopped and stared at that painting. "It's good, isn't it?" she said.

"Good?"

"I mean—it's good that they have each other. The girl

with four arms and the man with none. The mermaid and the alligator man. And these twins—they must never get lonely. It's good."

"I guess," I said. "I never thought about it like that."

When we turned and walked deeper into the fair, things got louder, wilder. People shouted from every booth, calling out the great value of their delicious treats or their spangled dancers. An organ grinder's tune competed with the songs from the bandstand, and kids rode around in circles on metal fire trucks, then stumbled off dizzy.

We watched a man hurl ball after ball at a pyramid of bottles, but try as he might, the bottles never fell. At last the man frowned and quit. The guy operating the game appeared to feel bad. He gave the loser a cigar and a pat on the back. But as the man walked away, I noticed there was a white handprint on the back of his shirt. I whispered to Molly, "What do you think *that* means?"

"I think it means we shouldn't try to knock over any bottles," she said.

Before long, we found ourselves in front of a stand where the smell of sugar was overpowering. It had been a while since breakfast.

"Cotton candy!" I said.

"What's that?" asked Molly.

"Straight sugar! Mom always says if I'm going to rot my teeth out, I might as well eat cotton candy and get it done fast. You have to try it!"

Molly laughed as a woman swirled a mass of whispery pink strands onto a paper cone. "We'll have one," she said eagerly to the woman, "to share." Then, with the candy in hand, she turned back to me and said, "I'd like to try everything!"

"Everything?"

Molly laughed. "I have a lot of catching up to do."

I grinned. "Lead the way."

First we made our way to the fried dough counter and bought one of those. Then we headed for the caramel popcorn stand, where we purchased a small paper bag of the treat.

"Hey, I'm going to drop something if I'm not careful," I said. "How about I sit down over . . ." I turned around in a circle, looking for a good place to sit. "There!" I motioned with my head to an old tree with a tangled system of roots.

Molly nodded, and then ran off. She bought a hot dog, a lemonade, and a candy apple. One at a time she deposited them with me, until I was surrounded by an amazing junkfest. All of it identical to the fair food back home, in 1987.

I resisted the impulse to start eating until Molly came back, holding something funny. "What's that?" I asked.

Molly shrugged. "I don't know what *most* of these things are," she said. She handed me the item in question, which appeared to be half a lemon with a broken candy cane jammed in it, then reached for the popcorn.

"What do I do with it?" I asked, nibbling at the rind and making a face.

Molly sat down. "Eat it, I suppose."

"Eat a raw lemon?" I wrinkled my nose.

That was when a high voice piped up from behind the tree. "A lemon stick. Ain't yous guys never seen a lemon stick?" A small face peered out at us from a long fall of dirty blond hair, and then a body in a stained dress joined the face. The girl looked six. "You suck it, like a straw."

"Like this?" I asked. I put my mouth on the top of the broken candy cane and drew a long gulp. My mouth shot through with a zing of cold mint and tart lemon. "Yow!" I grinned.

"Yer welcome," said the girl, her hands behind her back, eyeing our feast.

Molly, the candy apple stuck to her front teeth, looked the girl up and down. "Would you like something?" she asked the kid.

A smile split the girl's face. "Would I ever!" she shouted, squatting down and grabbing for the fried dough. "Thanks, lady!"

I laughed. "She called you *lady*."

In about two seconds, the dough was gone.

"Oh!" said Molly, setting down her apple. "Would you like another?"

The girl's eyes widened. "My sister would too, I bet! She's Olivia. I'm Annika. We're twins. Livi!"

From behind the tree another girl, identical to the first, popped out. "Yup?" They were like two really filthy elves.

"All right," said Molly. "Just wait. I'll be back before you can say 'Jack Robinson.' "

"Jack Robinson," I said. But the elves didn't laugh at my joke. They were too busy eating.

The girls gobbled up everything but my lemon stick, which I sucked slowly. By the time Molly returned, more dirty kids had joined us in the nest of tree roots. I wondered where their parents were. They looked awfully little to be alone.

"I suppose we'll need some more!" said Molly. She left again.

But while she was gone, a police officer strolled up. I could feel his shadow over me, even before I turned around. He wasn't the same guy from Woolworth's, of course, but it still made me nervous. His nose glistened in the summer sun as he squinted down at us.

"What've we got here, kids?" he asked. "What've you all been up to, hey?"

For no reason, my heart began to race. I wished Molly would hurry back.

"Nuffin," said Annika. "We ain't doin' *nuffin* wrong. These ladies just bought us lunch."

"They *did*, did they?" The policeman crossed his arms over his chest. "And where have you been getting all this money from, miss?" he asked me.

"I—umm." I looked up at his blue uniform, with all those shiny buttons, and though I knew we hadn't done anything wrong, I felt instantly flushed. Pictures flashed through my head of the smashing, crashing lamp disaster, and then of the girls' home. I gulped. "Umm. My friend has an allowan—"

Just then Molly returned with a plate of hot dogs in each hand. I scrambled to my feet and ran over to her. "Hey, Molly, I think it's time we left, don't you? We're . . . umm, meeting your mom at the Ferris wheel, remember?" I tried to wink so that the policeman wouldn't see me.

At first Molly was baffled. She looked at the policeman, and then at me. "But—but I wanted to try the cotton—"

I took the cone of cotton candy from the boy who'd buried his face in the sticky pink cloud. "Here you go," I said with a cheery fake smile, grabbing her hand. Hot dogs fell to the ground and rolled from their buns. I ignored them.

"All right, all right," said Molly as she let me push her. "Goodbye, everyone, goodbye!" She waved to all the other kids as we walked away. They scurried to pick up the hot dogs.

The policeman watched us walk away. Each time I turned to look back over my shoulder, he was still there, staring at me. I willed myself to face forward as we made our way to the Ferris wheel, bought our tickets, and climbed into the hot metal bucket.

Once we were up in the sky, with the fair spread out below us, I lost sight of him, and everything melted away. It was just me and Molly, our legs dangling over the booths and the water. It was like any Ferris wheel, every Ferris wheel. It was like the Georgia State Fair, with Mom. We rocked back and forth, and the bucket rocked with us.

"Look." Molly pointed at Annika and Olivia off in

the distance, beneath their tree. We rode up and down and around and around.

After the Ferris wheel, we wandered for a bit. A lot of the fair was just beer tents and grown-ups dancing, which didn't interest us. As the church bells above us rang out, we realized it was time to meet Frank. Of course, *that* was when we passed a small tent that made us stop and stare. Sitting in front of the tent flap was a table covered in tiny glass bottles and a sign that read:

FORTUNATA'S TEMPLE OF KNOWLEDGE:
POTIONS, PROPHESIES AND PREDICTIONS!
QUESTIONS ANSWERED. MYSTERIES REVEALED.
SETTLE YOUR HEART.

As we stood there, a man stepped from inside the tent. "May I help you?" he asked.

Fortunata wasn't what I'd expected at all. I'd pictured an old Gypsy-looking lady with big earrings and loads of black eyeliner, not a young man in a neat gray suit. He was clean-shaven, with soft brown hair and kind eyes. The air around him was quieter somehow. He gave a shy smile from beneath the brim of a squashed hat. In his hand he held a large white flower, faded and dying, the petals spotted with tan and brown.

Molly looked at the flower. "What is it?" she asked as she neared his table. "What do you have there?"

"Just magic," said the man. He gave the flower a soft shake.

"*Real* magic?" Molly asked.

I watched Molly watch the man. He looked nice enough, but *Prophesies and Predictions*? It was like something from an episode of the *Twilight Zone* or *Alfred Hitchcock Presents*. Too much like a story to be real.

"Wait," he said. "Patience." In front of our eyes, he opened a bottle of silvery blue dust and sprinkled a pinch of it onto the flower. He closed his eyes and shook the blossom, and when he stopped, it didn't look so dead.

I blinked, rubbed my eyes, and stared again. Was it possible the brown spots and streaks were vanishing? They were! Right in front of my eyes. The flower in front of me now was perfect, pristine, white, and fresh, as though it had just been plucked. A few petals had fallen to the tabletop, but even those now gleamed.

"No *way*! How'd you do that?" I asked, looking from the man to the flower and back again. "What's the trick?"

The man's eyes were soft. "A trick is only a game you haven't figured out the rules to," he said in his calm voice.

"You want us to believe you have *real* magic, in bottles?" I said. "For sale?"

The man shrugged. "I don't *have* magic. Magic just *is*."

"What do you mean?" asked Molly.

"Magic is what people call it when the universe corrects itself and they happen to be watching. Sometimes *this*"—he held up the bottle—"can help."

"I don't understand," said Molly.

"Now and then," said the man, "a thing needs to happen so badly the universe decides to rearrange itself. People like to call such events evolutions or miracles, depending on who they are and what they profess to believe. But it's all the same. I prefer to call it magic."

"So if I wish for something, it could actually happen?" asked Molly.

"Why not?" said the man. "If you're wishing hard enough, and it's something you genuinely need, why wouldn't the universe set things to rights?" He winked and added, "It only takes faith. But for only one shiny half dollar, I can help your faith along."

"This is a scam," I said, tugging at Molly's sleeve. "Let's go."

She shook me off. "Does it only work on flowers?" she asked. "Or can it help other things?"

"A true wish can do anything," said the man. "If you need it, in your heart."

"Please," said Molly. "Speak plainly. We're in a hurry. I only want to know—can that dust make people better? Can it make *me* better?"

The man looked her straight in the eyes. "Better than what? *Better* depends on how bad things are."

I don't know why, but I got the chills when he said that. The man seemed nice enough, but there was something about his calm tone that made me nervous. "Let's *go*," I said. "We'll miss Frank. Please?"

Molly set down a big half dollar on the purple cloth and took the bottle. "Thank you, Fortunata," she said.

"Oh, you can call me Seymour," he said pleasantly.

Molly waved over her shoulder as we ran, but I reached up and grabbed her hand midwave and pulled her along with me faster. Through the brick streets and past the music and the booths, until we were back near the market and the smell of fish.

"Slow down." Molly laughed. "Frank will wait."

But I didn't feel like slowing down. Something about all the wishing talk had made me nervous. For the first time, I only wanted to be back, safe, in the hotel. Still holding hands, panting slightly, we pushed right through the market, past buckets of flowers and men in blood-stained butcher aprons. When we shot out on the other side, there was Frank's shiny black taxi. He leaned against his door, smoking a cigarette.

I was relieved to see him, a familiar face. Besides Molly and Nora, I guessed I knew Frank better than anyone in town at this point.

"Frank!" I called.

"Why, hey!" he shouted, jumping up and opening our door. "You made it!"

We walked around the car. Molly climbed up onto the running board and I followed her.

Frank tossed his cigarette into the street, slammed our door shut, climbed in, and stepped on the gas. The car sprang out into the brick road.

"How was the fair?" he asked. "Yous guys see anything good?"

"We *did*," said Molly. "We saw it *all*."

"Very nice, very nice," said Frank. "And where exactly do you want me to take you now?"

"The alley behind the Hotel Calvert," I said without thinking.

"The *alley*?" He turned around. "Really?"

"It's . . . umm . . . a shortcut to our house," I said.

Frank chuckled. "I don't even want to know what you girls are up to, do I?"

"Perhaps it's better if you don't," admitted Molly.

"Your money, ladies. Your choice." Frank whistled as he drove along.

Safe in the car, Molly cradled Fortunata's tiny bottle in her hands, then held it up to the sunlight streaming in the rear window. It dazzled. "Do you think I'm supposed to eat it?" she asked. "Or perhaps sprinkle it onto my skin, like he did with the flower?"

"I don't think you should do *anything* with it," I said. "*Definitely* don't eat it."

"But *you* saw what it did to the flower! It made it perfect."

"That was a *trick*," I said. "Don't you think if he really had a magical lifesaving potion, he'd be working at a hospital? Obviously I believe in magic. Just not the kind people sell in bottles. Seriously, that stuff could make you sick."

"I'm *already* sick," said Molly.

"Look," I said, turning to her. "I *know* you'll be fine without any stupid dust. You'll live a long time. You just have to believe me."

"But . . ."

"If *you're* sick, *I'm* sick, Molly. I have trouble breathing too. Do I need to eat blue sparkles? Don't *I* seem fine?"

Molly nodded slowly. "You do," she said. "You always do."

"So we wheeze. We shouldn't run up mountains. But we're in the same boat, Molly. Please trust me?"

I thought Molly would argue, but she didn't. She just said, "I *do*, Annie. I *do* trust you. If you really believe that I shouldn't try it, I won't."

"You mean that?"

"Truly," she said, slipping the bottle into her pocket.

· 15 ·

SNEAKYPIES

That night, when Nora came up with dinner, we were collapsed on the carpet with Friend, staring at the ceiling. The maid burst into laughter. "I won't ask what you've been up to," she said. "But you look like tired puppies."

"Oh, Nora!" said Molly, sitting up. "We *are* tired, but it was such a day! We went to a fair!"

"When you weren't here for lunch," said Nora, "I was a mite concerned. But I'm pleased you had a good day." She set down her tray and served us each a plate of something fishy. Without meaning to, I wrinkled my nose.

"Now, now," scolded Nora, "plenty of children would be delighted with a nice bit of fish. You two don't know how lucky you are."

A picture of Annika's and Olivia's grubby, hungry faces flitted through my brain. I felt instantly awful, and I forced down a bite of the fish as penance.

"That said," added Nora, "I have something else for you too. Look!" She ducked into the hallway and returned with a red metal box.

"What's *that*?" Molly asked.

Nora laughed. "Well, until today it was a bread box, but I don't want the kitten messing in the closet anymore. I thought this might be just the thing." She headed for the bathroom.

We followed and watched as she tilted the bread box onto its back, lifted the door to an open position, and set it on the floor. When I looked inside, I saw that the box was half full of ashes.

"How clever you are!" said Molly. "Thank you!"

Nora blushed. "Why, it's hardly anything. The hinges were broken and the kitchen was about to give it away, so I nicked it!"

Friend had followed us into the bathroom and was sniffing around the box. He hopped right in.

"He likes it!" cried Molly.

"Sure enough," said Nora. "He's a good boy. Now, how about we leave him to his business and you return to your supper. If you don't like hot fish, you certainly won't enjoy it cold."

Once Nora was gone, we ate our peas and rice and fed some of the fish to Friend, who was leaving sooty little paw prints all over. We got into our nightgowns, but Molly didn't drink her powder that night. She carried it into the bedroom and set it on her little table, but then she just stared at it.

"Don't you need it?" I asked, staring at the cloudy glass. "To sleep?"

Molly eyed the glass. "I'm not even certain why they give it to me. Usually everything is so dull, I'm happy to nod off. But since *you* arrived, I don't want to. Today I'd rather lie here and remember. What a grand afternoon! Wasn't it?"

"Yeah," I said. "Totally." I rolled onto my side. "But if we aren't going to sleep yet, let's do something else."

"What do you suggest?" asked Molly.

"We could read."

"I always read."

"We could talk."

"We're doing that right now!"

"Well, then *you* think of something," I said, poking her in the arm.

Molly pondered for a minute. "Do you know what I've always thought about doing? Ever since I've been stuck in here?"

"I can't possibly guess," I said.

"From my window I can see two little statues. . . ." Molly crawled from the bed and pointed at the dark yards below. "Of the Blessed Virgin. Over there. One is made of white plaster, and the other is painted blue. They belong to two very old women, who scrub them and plant flowers at their feet."

"Okay," I said. "So?"

"*So* . . . I've always thought it would be fun if one day they suddenly switched places in the night. So that the women would think . . ."

"Ooh!" I sat up fast. "They'd think it was a miracle! What a great idea."

Molly smiled. "I think maybe we should do *that*."

I was out of bed now too. "You mean it? Right now? You want to go sneaking around in the night to steal other people's Blessed Virgins?"

"You don't think it's wrong, do you? I mean it to make them happy."

"No, I totally get it. Sure."

Molly was bouncing on her toes. "Also, I want to go down in the dumbwaiter this time, so we can stop in the kitchen for a snack. Because that fish was . . ." She made a face like she smelled something bad. "*Not* delicious. Maybe we can find some chocolate chips. Maggie and Ginny steal them all the time."

"I'm *so* totally in," I said. "*All* in. If you're sure you're up for this."

Molly nodded. "I truly, truly am." She pushed a chair over to the ugly dog painting, climbed up, and swung out the picture. Then she gasped.

"What is it?" I said.

"I don't know," said Molly. She reached in and pulled out a piece of paper.

I leaned over her shoulder to read it. All the note said was "*BE CAREFUL, GIRLS!*"

"Oh," I said. "It's just Nora."

"Yes," said Molly. But her face looked serious. She folded the note carefully and slipped it into the pocket of her nightgown.

"What's the big deal?" I asked.

Molly smiled. "It means—she was *thinking* of us. She was *concerned*. Isn't that nice?"

"I guess so," I said.

"It is," said Molly. "It matters. Because . . . she cares."

Two minutes later we were inside the black box, crammed together, creaking our way slowly down. One of Molly's knees was digging into my back, and I could feel blisters burning into my palms from the rope. But it wasn't as hard going down as it had been going up, and I was excited. At last we reached the bottom. Molly pushed gently at the door. It opened. A sliver of light shone in from the kitchen.

I whispered, "Hey, how do you know nobody will be down here?"

"I *don't*," hissed Molly. "But supper is over, and it doesn't *look* like anyone is here, does it?" She swung the door open a little further, and we slipped down carefully onto a big wooden table, and then to the tile floor.

"It looks safe," said Molly.

"Now what?" I asked.

"Now we feast!" Molly leaned into a cupboard. "What would you like?"

"Ugh. Anything but fish," I said. "Or liver. So *grody*."

"*Grody?*"

"Yeah, like gross, disgusting."

"Grody," repeated Molly slowly.

"Hey, I know," I said. "Let's invent something. Our own secret recipe. My friend Susie and I do that sometimes when she sleeps over. See what you can find for ingredients, okay?"

"Yes, yes!" Molly was so excited, her curls were trembling.

We snooped around for a few minutes, opening drawers and cupboards. Molly found ginger cookies, and I discovered a jar of raspberry jam. Molly turned up a bowl of whipped cream in the icebox. There wasn't a chocolate chip to be seen, but there was homemade buttercream frosting. We put everything on the table and layered it all. A cookie, spread with jam and frosting, slathered with whipped cream, and topped with another cookie. Together we sat down on the floor, each of us holding a gooey, amazing sandwich.

"This is," I said, nibbling my treat sideways, "the yummiest thing ever."

"Eyefinkshowtooo," mumbled Molly through a huge mouthful. She was grinning. There was whipped cream on her nose. She swallowed. "What shall we call them?"

"I don't know," I said. "Molly and Annie's Delicious Cookie Delights?"

Molly shook her head. "No, that's too long."

"True," I said. "So *you* come up with a name, Miss Smarty."

She licked a finger and pondered the question. "They

should be called . . . Sneakypies," she said. "And they can only ever be eaten late at night, in secret!"

"Hey, that's pretty good." I laughed.

We sat and ate and chewed and munched, and licked the sides when the whipped cream dripped out.

"Oof," Molly said at last. "I'm stuffed!" She patted her stomach happily and groaned as she stood up. Then she walked over to the kitchen door and opened it just a crack.

"Me too," I said. "But we still want to do our secret switcheroo thing, right? How will we get outside?"

Molly didn't answer. Instead, with no warning at all, she pushed gently at the swinging kitchen door and took a step.

· 16 ·

THE FROZEN LAND OF LONG AGO

"What are you doing *now*?" I called after Molly.

She turned back and held up a finger to her lips. "Shhh! Come on. There's nobody about. Let's go!"

"Go where?" I asked.

"I want a key," said Molly. "To my room. So we don't have to sneak in and out anymore. See?"

I peeked over Molly's shoulder. Sure enough, the desk was empty, and behind it on hooks were rings and rings of keys. "I want a key," repeated Molly slowly. "This is *my* home. I should have one, shouldn't I?"

"I . . . guess," I said.

"Here I go," she said, stepping away from the safety of the kitchen and into the main lobby of the hotel. Just like that. The door swung behind her.

I watched through the crack in the kitchen door.

We'd been hiding so long it was strange to see her out in the open. It was like she was walking from a dark closet into a great big field or something. I held my breath.

Molly skated slowly away from me, in her sock feet and nightgown, across that broad expanse of marble. I hadn't seen the lobby in all its glory before, and it took my breath away. The chandelier cast a soft, glittering light. The piano was gleaming ebony. The leather chairs looked deep and soft. The paintings that decorated the room were set in huge gilded frames. There was a warm, golden sheen to the room, a richness.

Molly looked tiny and pale in that great huge place. She made it to the reception desk and went around to the key hooks. She climbed onto a stool and reached up. I watched a small hand stretch out and grasp at a key. Then she slipped down again and waved for me to come out.

"Annie, look!" she called in an excited whisper, waving her key in the air. Her voice echoed across the cavernous lobby. She started back toward me.

I began to push open the swinging kitchen door for

her, but a voice broke the calm, a cold voice, an angry voice. "Mary!" It was the sound of a whip cracking. I let the door fall back again and peered through the crack.

Molly's father strode into view. "Mary!" he said again. "Mary Moran! Just *what* do you think you are doing downstairs? Dressed in your nightclothes?"

Molly spun around near the bottom of the staircase. Her face was white. Her eyes were huge. "Papa," she bleated. "I—"

I could see the confusion on her face. It was like she was grasping for a story. Her eyes darted in my direction, but there was nothing I could do.

"I just—was hungry," she said. "So I—I thought—"

"You *thought*? Your job is not to think, but to do as you are *told*!"

A moment later another man in a tuxedo entered the room. "Everything all right in here, James?" he asked.

Mr. Moran's thunder died. He waved to the man and cleared his throat. "Just a second, Robert," he said. "I'll be right there! Have a drink on the house. I need to take care of a small matter. Nothing of import. No need for concern."

The other man walked back the way he'd come, and Molly's father's spoke again, in the same tone I'd heard from under the bed that morning. Stern, cold. He reached out and grabbed Molly's arm. "I have *no* patience for this," he said. "I do not know how you got down here, and I'm *not* pleased. I have work to do, and no time for personal matters. We have guests, and I cannot have you complicating things. McGhee!"

I watched from afar as Molly's face crumpled. It was like she shrank, faded.

From the staircase above, another man scurried down, a thin, nervous man in glasses. "Yes, sir? Did you need something, Mr. Moran?" When he saw Molly, his eyes went wide.

Molly's father looked up. "Yes, McGhee. You are to take my daughter back to her room immediately." He turned his back on Molly and started walking away. "I'll deal with her tomorrow. Also, please tell Nora I'll need to speak with her in the morning, first thing."

"Yes, sir," said McGhee, looking concerned as he continued swiftly down the stairs, his eyes on Molly.

Mr. Moran disappeared, and I heard the sound of a door shutting as McGhee reached out to Molly. Molly hung her head and turned to face him.

But suddenly—Molly changed. Her back straightened, her chin lifted, her arms rose, and she ran. Molly burst forward. At first I thought she was running at McGhee, charging him, but then I realized—no! Molly ran at the angel, the lovely marble angel on the pedestal at the foot of the stairs.

"It isn't *fair!*" she shouted, throwing up her hands, pushing at the base with all her might. "I *won't* go back!" The pedestal rocked, tipped slightly. "Why do you *hate* me so?" Molly called, pushing again. "Is it because I'm sick? *Why?*"

Slowly the pedestal tilted, and then the angel fell, crashing to the floor. Molly sank to her knees, surrounded by chunks of marble. She was wheezing hard, panting for air. Crying.

Through the crack in the door, I searched for Molly's father. I wanted him to run to her, to scoop her up like a baby and make everything okay. But he was nowhere to be seen. He'd left the room. He was already gone.

Molly began to cry quietly into her hands.

It hurt me to see her like that. She looked so alone, a pale tiny thing in that huge rich room. I had to keep myself from running to her, but what could I do? What would it help for me to get caught? Where would they take me? The Baltimore Home for Girls? I couldn't afford to find out.

McGhee knelt slowly and pulled Molly to her feet. He

looked upset. "Miss Moran," he said gently. "Molly, come along. You'll feel better in the morning." He wrapped an arm around her shoulders and led her to the elevator.

I don't remember backing away from the door or climbing up into the dumbwaiter. I don't know how I pulled myself back up to the seventh story on my own. But I must have done it slowly, because by the time I tumbled out and into bed, Molly was already asleep, drugged, breathing slow.

I didn't know what else to do, so I just crawled in beside her. I stared at Molly's flushed cheeks and watched the rise and fall of the covers as she snored. I pushed her hair out of her face. I felt so sad. I couldn't imagine what kind of trouble she'd be in tomorrow. What else could they possibly do to her? What was left for them to take away?

I turned over in the bed, thinking about what I'd witnessed, and my mind replayed the scene in the lobby. All that shouting. The angel falling. The crash! So loud. It was a shame. I'd liked the angel.

Then something clicked in my brain, and I sat back up. The angel. She wasn't *supposed* to smash. She was supposed to *be* there, waiting for me, dusty in the darkness. I'd touched her, or I *would* touch her, unbroken, in the future. Only now I couldn't. Now she couldn't greet me when I arrived. What did that mean? That things *could* be shattered! Things *could* be changed. *I* could change things.

I lay back, stared up at the canopy, and tried to think of what I might have already changed. Out of nowhere, a word hit me: *TEEVEESET!* I groaned, thinking of all the girls singing "Miss Lucy," even though there were no *teeveesets* in the world to sing about yet. The things happening all around me were not only in the past. This wasn't a vacation in the frozen land of long ago, a distant memory. These things were happening for real. What did that mean? Could they really change the future? Could they ruin it?

I *had* to go home, *now*! It *had* to work this time. I couldn't stay any longer. This was too much. If only it would work this time . . . I reached under the bed for the mask.

But the mask wasn't there! So I climbed down from the bed and crawled under to look. Over by the wall, I saw something crumpled . . . the mask! I reached out to grab it and breathed a sigh of relief when my fingers fell on heavy silk. But as I was backing out from under the bed, I saw something else crumpled in the darkness and reached for that too. I recognized the feel of it, the stretched elastic, the loose beads.

I stood up and stared at the two objects in my hands, puzzling. *Two* masks? Both of them lost beneath the bed. One mask was Molly's—new and shiny and forgotten before I'd even arrived. One mask was mine—faded and falling to pieces, stolen from the future. The masks were the same, and yet they were different. I tried to understand. . . .

Did this mean anything?

Maybe it did! Maybe it meant I'd been using the wrong mask.

Hope fluttered inside me. Maybe *this* was the answer! Maybe this was why the mask hadn't worked for me. Because it hadn't been my mask! It had been Molly's. Maybe now that I had my mask back, everything would be fine.

It *had* to. I willed it to. Because if things were changing in the past, I had no way of knowing what they'd do to my future. Maybe I was losing my memories each morning because those moments were actually disappearing. My stomach lurched just thinking about it, and I lay back down in the bed. I needed to get home *now*, while it was still there. I slipped on the mask, *my* mask, the right one this time. I hoped.

I held my breath as I pulled the mask down and waited. For something, anything, to happen. For a moment, with my eyes squeezed shut beneath the silk and my mind focused on Mom, with my fingers crossed and my heart hopeful, I felt a twinge, a lifting, a half beat.

But it faded.

No.

No!

The magic didn't come. No static. No strange silence. Just the sound of Molly snoring. Just my thoughts, still there, licking like flames at the edges of my sleep. I held my breath and counted to ten. I wanted to sleep. I wanted to run away from everything. Even Molly.

But it did no good.

I reached up and touched the sleeping mask on my eyes lightly.

I wanted to cry.

· 17 ·

UNNECESSARY EMOTIONS

When I woke up the next morning, I felt sad. At first I didn't know why. Then I pulled off my mask, looked at Molly, and remembered.

Her father. The angel. There was no fog around those memories. I didn't have to work to know where I was. I remembered the shattering, the fight.

But when I tried to push further, the fog was back. It took many seconds before the rest came, dragging itself like a broken leg. Some part of me recalled this feeling of being lost, of waking in a cloud, and I just lay there, waiting for things to get better.

I struggled, casting about for the pictures, the words, until like a cloud taking shape, it arrived—a picture of a woman with short brown hair and a smear of lipstick. With that memory came more sadness.

Bit by bit I brought it all back to me. But there was no joy in the remembering. It was painful, to think I had to work at remembering Mom. *Chicken pox. SpaghettiOs.* I pulled out stories. *Brown bag lunches with cartons of chocolate milk. Smurfs.* All of it like a story I'd read, all of it distant and sad.

Eventually Molly woke and rolled over too. She stretched. She stared at me. She rubbed her eyes. "McGhee took my key," she said.

I reached out a hand to touch her arm. "Are you okay?" I asked.

"I think so," she replied. She picked at the bedspread for a minute, and then she shot me a strange look.

"I lied to you," she said.

"About what?"

"My father. He *is* mean."

"Oh, that. Well, all parents suck sometimes," I said.

"Is *suck* a bad thing?" Molly asked.

I nodded.

"Then yes. They do *suck*. I didn't want to say it before. Perhaps I thought that would make it more real, saying it out loud. He's always been cold to me, but this summer . . . I've just been up here alone, waiting for things to be better. Instead they got worse. Papa *sucks* terribly, and if he's going to hate me, then maybe I can just hate him back. That might be easier."

"Hold the phone," I said. "What are you talking about? *Hate?* He doesn't *hate* you."

"How can you say that?" asked Molly. "He locks me away in here."

"You're wrong," I said, shaking my head. "He's a jerk, sure, but he doesn't *hate* you. He's your dad. He put you up here because some doctor told him it was what you needed. And he's ignoring you because he's a dumb grown-up. That's what they do half the time, ignore us."

"But *your* mother doesn't. You said she was *plenty*. Remember? You said she was *there*."

"Well, she is, but that doesn't mean she isn't a screwup! I also told you she forgets to pick me up from dance class, remember? One year she forgot my birthday, and she's the worst tooth fairy on the planet. Also, she's kept secrets from me all my life, about some pretty important stuff."

"What sort of secrets?"

"Oh—umm, stuff about my grandma. But never mind about her. You wouldn't be interested. The point is—parents can be stupid and mean, but that doesn't mean they don't love us."

"He's always busy." Molly shook her head. "*Always*."

"I don't know, Molly. Maybe your parents are fighting. Maybe that's why your mom is gone right now. Hey, if this were a movie, he'd have a mortal illness or a drinking problem. But he does love you. Even when they're being mad or dumb, your parents *have* to love you. It's in their DNA or something."

Molly stared at me. "What's DNA?"

"Never mind. Just be glad you've *got* parents."

Molly rubbed her wet eyes on her sleeve. When her face came away from the fabric, she looked slightly less miserable. "You know—I don't exactly believe what you said, but I'd like to. I want to. Perhaps—I *need* to."

Nora didn't show up that morning with breakfast. Nobody did. Molly and I sat and waited. We got hungry. We played a game of checkers and tried not to think about muffins. Friend roamed around mewing. He'd gotten used to his sardines.

At last Molly's belly growled so loud I could hear it. "Oh my!" she said. Her cheeks turned pink. "Excuse me."

"No problem," I said. "I'm starving too. My stomach feels like it's been scraped out like a jack-o'-lantern."

"Mine feels like a cave," said Molly miserably. She pushed away the checkerboard. "Come on!" She headed for the bathroom.

We made our way down the fire escape, carefully because we were feeling so faint. But at the bottom, instead of heading to the alley or the basement, Molly turned sharply and walked up the path to the front of the hotel, right around the side of the building to the main drive. I followed her as she marched in through the double doors.

I hung back by the piano as Molly went up to the reception desk and rang the brass bell. I had no idea what to expect. "Papa!" she called. "Is my father here? McGhee!"

After a minute Mr. McGhee appeared.

"Yes," he said nervously from behind the desk. "Oh! Miss Molly. You're . . . back. I didn't expect you. Your father is, erm, occupied. Are you supposed to be downstairs? I've grown unaccustomed to seeing you about." Mr. McGhee looked like he might throw up. He kept fidgeting with his glasses.

Molly cleared her throat. "Where is he?"

"He's in his office . . . taking care of a business matter."

McGhee ran his hand through the wisps of hair on his head. "Nothing you need concern yourself with. But if I might ask . . . how did you get out?"

"Fire escape," Molly said simply as she turned away.

Mr. McGhee stared after her and said nothing as Molly walked to a large door, which she pulled open without knocking. The door was so big she had to tug at it with both hands. I followed, lingering at the open door.

Inside the office Mr. Moran was standing behind a large desk. Facing him sat Nora in a straight-backed chair. Mr. Moran was glaring at her. As Molly entered, he looked up in surprise. "Mary," he said in his grim voice. "I have had quite enough of your shenanigans."

When Molly cut her father off, what came out of her was a voice so remarkably like Mr. Moran's that I caught my breath. "No," she said coldly. "No, you really *haven't* at all! Now listen to me!"

Nora stared wide-eyed at Molly. Then she turned back to Mr. Moran.

I waited at the door, afraid to enter. I didn't have a place in that room.

Mr. Moran's voice was a growl now. It reminded me of teeth grinding. "And just what is it you expect me to listen to, Mary? This is not the time."

Molly spoke sharply. "It's *never* the time for me, Papa.

Ever." Molly was mad. But there were tears in her eyes too. "I can't stay there anymore, in the Lonely Room. It's too horrible, and look at me! I'm fine, I *am*."

"You are *not* fine," said Mr. Moran, glaring at his daughter. "I apologize if I haven't come to see you as I ought, if I haven't done my duty. I've been busy. But you are not well, and you can't be running around this way. I thought Nora could keep an eye on you, but I suppose we need someone stricter to—"

"No!" cried Molly. "It's not Nora's fault. She's been wonderful."

Mr. Moran tossed a hand into the air, exasperated. "*Just* like your mother, full of unnecessary emotions. I have no time for this. McGhee!"

"Papa. Please. Listen? You don't have to visit me, or talk to me, or love me, but don't make Nora go. I need her. I need . . . *someone*." The tears spilled over now.

Mr. Moran looked like he'd been socked in the gut. "What? What did you just say?"

Molly stuttered through her tears. "P-p-please don't make Nora go."

"No. Did you just say . . . I don't *love* you?"

Molly didn't speak, only nodded. Her crying was silent. "It's all right. I understand. Just leave me Nora. Please?"

For a minute Molly and her father just looked at each other. His hands were on his desk, as though holding him up. Molly was shaking, alone, in the middle of the room.

"I *don't*," he said.

"Don't?" Molly tilted her head and said it again. "Don't?"

"I don't . . . *not* love you."

"*Really?*" Molly's voice rose hopefully.

Mr. Moran sat down in the big chair. "I *care* for you, don't I? Keep you fed and clothed? Call the doctor? Provide dolls and games and so forth?"

"Dolls, yes," Molly said quietly. "I have dolls . . . and plenty of *pudding*."

Nora stifled a sob.

"But I'm *alone*, Papa," said Molly at last. "*Always* alone."

Mr. Moran put a hand to his face. "It's what the doctor said you needed."

"He was *wrong*," Molly replied fiercely. "I *know* he was."

Her father took a deep breath. "Mary, when I was a boy, we lived in two rooms, ten of us. I shared a bed with my three brothers. My parents sent me to work in a factory. When I made my money, then married your mother and came to own all this"—he gestured at the rich room—"I swore my children would never live like that, never."

"But—"

"I never thought, in all my days, that a child with everything might feel . . . unloved."

That was when I really thought they might hug and kiss. In a movie that would have happened. But all Molly did was take a deep breath. Her tears had dried. She wasn't shaking anymore. "I understand. I do. And if you would let Nora stay, I'll go back to my room. For now."

Mr. Moran looked very tired. "I'm sorry, but I think that would be best. I have work to do. Work cannot be set aside, not even for one's children. You understand?"

"I think I do," Molly said. "Yes."

"But," said Mr. Moran, "you must promise you'll not go running around in the night anymore, or climbing through windows. Can you do that? And in exchange, perhaps Nora can bring you down into the yard each day. And for meals. You do seem . . . improved."

"Oh, I am, Papa, I promise I am!"

"I suppose we should also find you a key to your room," said Mr. Moran. "How would that be?"

Molly nodded. She turned to go. Nora rose too.

Mr. Moran cleared his throat. "I wonder, Molly, have you had breakfast?" he asked.

"No—no, sir," she said.

"Perhaps you should go do that," said Mr. Moran. "It's important to eat." He smiled at her. It was a small smile, but a real one. "I suggest you have waffles. They're my personal favorite."

Molly smiled back. "Yes, *sir*," she said. "I'll do just that!"

· 18 ·

A FEATHERY FEELING

Everything in the coffee shop was small. The white leather swivel stools were low, and the glasses of water were like children's cups. It all made me feel very big, like I might knock something over.

Molly smiled shyly as she sat down. "I'm not exactly certain what just happened," she said. "I can't believe it did. Pinch me?"

"You were brave," I said.

"I didn't have any other choices. I *had* to do that. It was as though it all happened *to* me."

From behind the counter, a waitress arrived and set

down two small cups of coffee, a cream pitcher, and two tiny spoons. "Why, Miss Molly! I haven't seen you in months and months. We heard you were poorly. Doing better?"

"I am, Irma, thank you." Molly nodded cheerfully, then looked back at me. "Would you like waffles?" she said. "Papa's right. They're very good."

"Sure, I guess," I said. The waitress made a note and hurried off.

I stirred cream into my coffee and took a sip. It was bitter. Mom didn't let me have coffee. I looked at the tiny spoon, fingering raised letters that said HC on the silver handle. "Pretty," I said. It was heavier than it looked.

"My sisters and I used to steal those," said Molly. "For tea parties." She spun her stool. "Oh, it *does* feel nice to be out and about, not having to sneak anymore. It's been over a year since I got to come down here for breakfast. Isn't this fun?"

I didn't know what to say. I was glad for Molly, but I was still stuck. What would happen to me now? What could happen when Mr. Moran found out about me? I thought again of the girls' home, of Bayla. I couldn't sort it out. My brain felt like a TV on the fritz, full of buzz.

Then the waffles arrived, each with its own tiny pitcher of syrup. Molly smeared soft butter on hers and began to cut fiercely and cram bites into her mouth. "So what shall we do today?" she asked through a sticky mouthful.

"I don't know," I said. I watched her lick her fork happily. "I guess we should stay in. You just promised your dad—"

"Well," she said, "I only said I wouldn't run around at *night*, or climb through *windows*."

"Oh, okay," I said. "I guess."

"You know what?" she asked.

"Uh-uh, what?"

"Someday I'm going to be a grown-up, and I won't be like Papa. I mean to have lots of children, so that I can tell them all the time how much I love them."

It made me happy to hear Molly talking so cheerfully about the future, but it also gave me a shiver. I thought of Mom. "Maybe you'll just have *one* kid," I said. "That would be okay, right?"

"I suppose," said Molly, taking a sip of water. "But who only has one child?"

"Well, my mother," I said. "I'm all she has. And she was an only child too."

"I've been an only child for one month. It hasn't been nice at all."

I shrugged. "Mom and I do lots of fun things together. Road trips and dinners out and stuff. It's . . . nice." I stared at the remains of my waffle.

Molly set down her fork. "Are you all right, Annie?" she asked.

"I don't know," I said. "I miss her. And I'm getting . . . scared."

Molly thought about that, licking a drip of syrup from her finger. "Perhaps we should go back to the fair. You could ask Mr. Fortunata what to do."

"Don't be silly," I said. "How can he help me?"

"I don't know," said Molly. "But wouldn't doing *something* be better than doing *nothing*?"

I thought about that. "Yes, *something*. I guess."

"Then it's settled," said Molly. "We'll go back to the fair. And we'll take all my money, so that on our way back, we can pay for the lamps. Everything will work out just right. Right?"

When we were finished with our waffles, I followed Molly over to Mr. McGhee's desk, where she grinned as she took the key from him. Then we scurried upstairs for Molly's money, and to say a quick hello to Friend before we rode back downstairs and cut through the grand lobby, heading for the big double doors. They were held open for us by two men in green and gold uniforms.

"Bye, Joe! Bye, Quincy!" Molly called lightly over her shoulder. She was grinning as she stepped into the circular drive, where a taxi just happened to be waiting. I ran down the steps after her.

I climbed into the car, half expecting to see Frank Callahan again. Instead our driver was an older man. He looked back over his shoulder. "And where will we be heading today, miss?" he asked in a formal tone.

When Molly said, "To the market in Fell's Point, please," the driver didn't comment. He drove in silence. It felt distant, cold. Very different from our speedy cruise with Frank.

As we pulled up near the harbor, I tried to be hopeful. But the day was chillier. I noticed how old the boats were. I saw how all the masts stabbed at the gray sky. The water was choppy and oily. The docks were dirty.

We climbed out of the taxi, paid the silent driver, and walked toward the fair. Molly looked loose and easy in her skin. I wished I could be easy in mine. But what if I never made it home? I pictured Mom, driving the streets of Baltimore alone, fifty years away. Mom, heading home to Atlanta by herself. Would she *do* that? I guessed she'd have to eventually. The same way everyone survived things. Molly in her Lonely Room. Bayla at the home.

Could *I* survive it? Never going home, being without Mom? I had a feathery feeling in my belly when I thought about it, a flurry of panic. I walked faster.

Then for some reason Fortunata's words swam back to me: "Magic is what people call it when the universe corrects itself." I thought about those words, and for the first time I considered that maybe I was just part of *Molly's* story, Molly's wish. She seemed so much better. Maybe I was only here to help correct things for her.

I stopped walking, frozen by the thought. So many things had changed because I was here. The angel had broken and wouldn't be there for me to find back in the future. Molly was not going to spend years in her Lonely Room. She might become a different person altogether.

Would I stay, stranded forever? Was it possible that the past—*this* past—might be my life now? Maybe the fog would get a little heavier each morning until I didn't notice anymore. What then?

What if Molly moved to China and never met my grandfather, whoever he was? What if she became a nun, or had all those kids she wanted? What if none of those kids was my mom? The feathers of fear rose up from my belly into my throat. For a block I couldn't breathe.

And what about Mom? In that other future, where Molly escaped the Lonely Room, would Mom exist at all?

Oh, god. It made a terrible kind of sense.

I walked beside Molly in silence, thinking, *There has to be a way. . . . There has to be a way.* We turned away from the harbor and market into the fair, and I began to run. Molly chased after me and we ran on those rough bricks, with the breeze from the water on our faces. At last we slowed. My cheeks were hot. Molly was panting from her run, wheezing again, and so was I.

We stopped in front of the cotton candy booth. "I can't remember," I panted, "exactly where he was. Do you?"

Molly looked around. "I'm certain he was over here, this way!"

We walked where Molly had pointed, and I saw things I hadn't noticed the day before. There was a man on a bench, asleep, drooling on his own arm. I noticed ragged hems on the colorful costumes the dancing girls wore. There was peeling paint and trash on the ground. Suddenly something seemed wrong about a flock of too-skinny people waiting to see a fat lady.

At last we arrived in front of Fortunata's booth. He was cutting up an apple. "You've returned," he said pleasantly. "I hope you were satisfied with your purchase."

"Yes!" said Molly. "Or . . . no. Well, I haven't tried it yet. But I feel better."

"That's all that matters," said the man. "Apple?" He held out a slice.

"Oh, no, thank you," said Molly.

"You?" He held out the slice to me, and I took it

silently as I tried to sort out what to say. I watched the man take a bite. After he swallowed, he said to me, "So, then, it's *your* turn, is it?"

"I . . . yes!" I said, startled. "How did you know?"

"Process of elimination," said the man.

"Oh, well, I mean, I doubt you can help. But I—"

He spoke softly. "If you *doubt* I can help, I can't. What is it you need?"

"I'm not sure how to explain it," I said. "It's complicated."

"Try," he said.

"Well, I need . . ." I faltered. "I need to find . . . my future."

He looked at me, staring deep. His eyes were a warm greenish brown, a comforting, earthy color. "Your *future*? You're certain about that?"

I nodded. "I'm sure."

"In that case," he said, setting down his apple, "show me your palm."

I glanced at Molly nervously, then slid my trembling hand into his still one. The man lowered his eyes, stared down a minute, then looked up. His face had gone pale.

"What?" I asked, petrified. "What *is* it?"

"No." He dropped my hand. "*This* I can't do." He took a step backward. "It's too much."

"Why? What's the matter?" asked Molly.

"Wait," I insisted. "Please *tell* me. What's going to happen?"

"I don't know," he said, shaking his head. "You are *between* futures. I think you already know that. Don't you?"

I nodded.

"I *can* tell you that all will be well," said the man, "no matter what may come. The world will keep turning. You will have good days and bad, wherever you are, whoever you are. Can you take comfort in that? Is it enough?"

I shook my head. There were tears waiting behind my eyes, burning. "It isn't."

"Oh, dear," he said. He looked genuinely sorry.

"I just want my mom," I choked out. "That's the only thing I want in the world."

"If that's true," said the man earnestly, "then focus on that. Don't look away; don't forget it. The more you care about something, the more you *need* it . . . the more likely you are to make it real. Do you understand?"

I nodded again. "I just want to be *sure*. If you could promise me that everything would turn out, it would be so much easier to believe. . . ."

"Ahh, but you've got it backward," said the man as he ducked inside his tent. "*You* have to believe. Until you do . . . anything can happen."

· 19 ·

LIKE A BRUISE

Annie?" Molly reached out and placed a hand on my arm. "Are you all right?"

I brushed her hand off and dropped to the grimy curb, staring at my scuffed Mary Janes. Inside I was shaking. "No," I said softly.

"What's wrong?" She knelt beside me in the street. "You're so . . . different all of a sudden. I wish I could help. I *want* to help."

"He said anything can happen," I murmured darkly.

"What?" Molly asked. "What did you say?"

I looked up into her eyes. "*Anything* can happen."

I was almost shouting now. "Anything! Do you get it?"

"I'm trying," she said softly. "I really am."

"I just want to go home." I threw a rock into the street.

Nothing had actually changed since yesterday, but everything was wrong. I felt like screaming. I did *not* feel like trying to explain something I didn't understand to Molly.

When she sat down beside me, I stood up and began walking again. "Wait!" Molly called from behind me. "Annie, wait! You're going too fast."

I turned back and saw she was panting, clutching her chest. Of course she was. None of this was her fault. I knew that. But she was here, and Mom wasn't. She was better, and I . . . might never be.

"Annie!" called Molly again. "Please? Don't leave me!"

I took a deep breath and trudged back to where Molly was bent over. I watched her wheeze. "I'm just going to find us a taxi." I scowled. "Stay here."

She rose. "No. I'm all right now. I can keep up."

We started moving again, together. We walked in silence, away from the water. The houses were dingy. A few cars passed us, but no taxis. We couldn't see the water anymore, and I had no idea where we were.

Then a raindrop fell.

I picked up my pace as more drops fell.

"Great!" I shouted miserably as I ran. "C'mon, run, Molly!" Molly tried to keep up, sprinting beside me. When would we see a taxi?

In the distance, out over the water, there were big ugly clouds spreading toward us like a bruise. As rain spattered down and the bricks grew wet under my feet, I thought of Mom, fifty years in the future, fumbling at the hotel door. I ran another block. I was soaked.

Behind me, Molly called my name.

Without turning my head, I called out, "What is it?"

"Should we find some cover?" she asked.

I just kept running.

"Please, Annie!" Molly called. "What's wrong? Why won't you talk to me?"

I still didn't stop.

"Annie!" she shouted. "Let's wait out the rain, okay?"

I didn't turn back. I let loose and ran. It hurt, and *that* felt good. My heart thumping, my head pounding, the rain spitting around me, and my feet beating the rough bricks. *Take that, take that, take that.* I didn't know what would happen, but as long as I was running, I couldn't stop to think. . . .

The rain came harder. My braid had come undone

and my hair was streaming down my back. Then I hit a loose brick and almost fell. I stopped to catch my breath. I could see Molly far behind, but my vision was blurry. I rubbed my eyes. I was dizzy. I was panting too hard. So I sat down, there in the rain. I was so wet, it didn't matter. I waited to catch my breath, for the rain to stop. For Molly to catch up.

Now I was wheezing badly. I'd never breathed so hard sitting still. I hiccupped and gasped, and I couldn't tell what was asthma and what was me trying not to cry. But I couldn't stop any of it. The ragged gasping and my ragged wish for Mom, all mixed up together. I closed my eyes.

That was how Molly found me. She knelt beside me, in my puddle. She looked into my face, and I saw her fear. "Why didn't you slow down?" she shouted, wiping the wet hair from my face.

I could only shake my head. I was racked by a spasm. *This* wasn't supposed to happen to me. Molly was the sick one.

"I'll get help," she said. She stood and ran to a house, banged on the door, but nobody came. Thunder crashed. The afternoon was dark as dusk.

Molly ran back to me. "We haven't time to waste," she said. "Come on." She began to pull me, to tug at my arm.

"We'll find a taxi," she was saying. "We'll get you safe." Molly held my hand. She dragged me to my feet. I stumbled after her.

The rain came on harder, but we walked slowly. Molly pulled my arm around her neck, and I leaned against her. I could feel her thin shoulder tremble under my weight. We kept our faces down. The thunder was loud above. We trudged through the puddles, holding each other, soaked to the bone. It was hard to tell the mud from the horse poop. I didn't even care.

For a minute I was breathing better, wheezing less. After several blocks of narrow dark streets, we turned onto a wider avenue and ducked under a tree. It wasn't enough to keep us dry, but the drops came slower there. Still no taxis passed. Molly let go of my arm and walked away.

For a second I thought she was ditching me. Then she turned and stood right in the middle of the avenue, waiting. At last a car came, swerved to miss her, and kept on going. Then another, which splashed through a puddle and covered her with mud. At last one honked and slowed. "Crazy kid!" shouted a voice through a window.

"Please, sir, we need a ride!" Molly shouted. "My friend is sick."

"You're wet!" yelled the driver.

"I have forty-three dollars!" Molly screamed.

The car rolled to a stop, and a minute later we were in it.

I lay on the seat, clutching my chest, dripping and gasping and grateful. I looked up at Molly. She was wheezing too.

"Jinx?" she asked.

I tried not to laugh. It hurt to laugh. "Jinx," I whispered.

As the car rumbled along, I felt myself calming, slowing. I was catching my breath. I was breathing. It would be okay. It would all be okay.

At last we were pulling up in front of the hotel. Molly shoved her entire bundle of money at the man. Then we were in the elevator, heading up to our room. After that, Molly was stripping off my wet dress, helping me into the bed. She was tucking me in.

"You're much better," she said. "Still, I'll go for the doctor. Will you be okay, for just a minute, alone? I promise I'll be quick."

I nodded.

I heard her walk away, and as she opened the door, she said, "It's so strange, Annie. Seeing you like this is like seeing *me*, almost. I wish I could help you. It doesn't feel fair. You've helped me, and now I want *you* to be better. I want you to be happy. More than anything in the world."

I lay there in the darkness and felt my chest rise and fall. "I'll survive," I panted.

"I know you will," she said. It sounded like the truth.

"Molly," I wheezed painfully. "How will you pay for the lamps . . . now?"

"Just rest," she said. "I'll be back with Dr. Irwin."

I nodded, and the door shut.

I was alone. Breathing hard.

I lay in that big bed and found myself awash in memories, all the details I'd been afraid to lose in my fog each morning. Mom, the smell of her Pert shampoo, her loud laugh. The way she chewed her fingernails at the exact moment she was telling me not to bite mine. Her straw purse slung over one shoulder. The mini Snickers bars she hid from me in the freezer. All the things I thought I'd forgotten. They calmed me, those thoughts. Mom letting me steer the car while she put on lipstick. Mom throwing a Rubik's Cube out the kitchen door when she couldn't finish it. Mom singing me to sleep.

After a few minutes Friend curled up on my chest and purred into my wet skin, the nook of my neck. He rubbed my face, concerned. It felt nice to have him there as he butted his little head into my cheek, my nose, my mouth.

Until . . . something happened.

One minute I was remembering, and feeling that

warm furball against my face, and the next I had a tickle in my throat. Then I couldn't breathe. I couldn't get a breath, not one. It wasn't like I was gasping; it was like I *couldn't* gasp. I threw a hand up, but there was nobody to see it.

I sat up and opened my eyes, looking wildly around the room. Where was Molly? I pushed Friend off me, and then stumbled to the bathroom, turned on the shower, and tried to breathe in the hot wet air. It wasn't enough.

I opened the medicine cabinet, looking for something, anything, wishing for my inhaler, but there was nothing.

Then I saw it—the blue bottle, the dust I didn't believe in. The poison. Shining on the top shelf. I was out of air, out of time. There was nothing left to lose. I opened the bottle, tipped it back, and then . . . I felt a giant spasm rack my body, and the dust went flying, spilling blue into the cat box at my feet.

I would have shouted, but there was no air for shouting. I could only think my shout. With a stabbing pain in my chest, I dropped to the floor. And as the lightning flashed, and the lights went out, and the world spun into darkness, I took one last try for a breath. Alone. I was so alone.

I wish, I thought to myself as my eyes fluttered. *I wish*

I wish I wish I wish I wish I wish for Mom, for Mom, for Mom, I need my mom.

Then a clap of thunder tore the night and trembled my darkness.

And then.

Light, blinding. It hurt my eyes.

"Annie, kiddo! Here, breathe deep."

I sat up, gasping, clutching, grabbing at air. I was sprawled on cold white tile. My stomach lurched, and when I saw her . . . I burst into tears.

There she was. *Here* she was. At last.

With a robe around me, and in her hand something plastic, purple, my inhaler, a tube of breath, a godsend, tasting of perfume and hair spray and medicine. I was breathing and crying and crying and breathing, sucking it in, all of it. Mom and the air and the *now*, home. Everything was expanding, my lungs so big they could take in the world. Every breath, shuddering with tears. I wanted every breath. All of them. I sobbed and collapsed back onto the tile.

Mom dropped too, sitting on the floor beside me. She was holding me, pulling me into her lap. I was crying, and she was saying, "Shhh, shhh, it's okay. Honey. Honey. You're fine."

And I settled into calm. Shhh. Shhh. I *was* fine. I was safe, and home. I was back and the rain was still beating against the window. It was as if I'd never left. One long crazy night.

Only then *she* was sobbing. Mom.

She tried to stop herself at first, raising a hand to cup her face, but her fingers were over her eyes and her face was buried in my hair and I could feel her tears, her shaking. We were just like that, a mess, a family. I buried my face in her T-shirt. I felt like my body was coming apart at the seams, flying into pieces. I was in her lap. Too big, spilling out, but I needed to be there.

Mom leaned over me, resting her head on mine, and a wrenching cry ripped from her. An animal sound. Her chest heaved. Her body shook.

"It's okay. I'm fine now," I said. "I can breathe. I promise." I looked up and took a deep breath. "See? You don't have to worry. I'm fine."

"I know, kiddo," Mom whispered. Then she shuddered. "But sh-sh-sh-sh-she's still g-g-g-gone!"

She?

Oh! *She.*

I reached up and pushed her hair from her face, saying, "It's okay. It'll be okay."

"She's gone. She's gone, and I—I—I'm an orphan

now," Mom cried in a heaving voice. "Isn't that f-f-funny? I keep thinking that. Can grown-ups be orphans?" She started to wipe her face with her sleeve.

I remembered *that*, that gesture, a sleeve wiping a tearstained face. Automatic. I remembered—Molly! Then all through me came a deep, slow ache. A heavy mourning, as I understood what had happened. What had *just* happened. Molly . . . was gone.

I was here, was home, had made it, but she—

Tears started to roll down my face again, but now I was crying with my mother. We were together in our sadness, crying for two people, a girl and a woman.

Molly was gone, dead, cold. In the next room. In 1987. Where she belonged. It was okay. It was the *right* end. It was time, and yet, in a wash of fuzzy memories, it felt as if someone had wrenched me from a dream.

"I'll miss her," I said. "I'll miss her so much, Mom."

"I know you will, kiddo," said my mom, straightening up. "We all will. She was an amazing woman."

I nodded my wet face. But then I sat up. Because—what about the dandelion clock, the smile like a knife? "She—she *was*? Amazing?"

Mom laughed, a laugh with a sob stuck in it. "You have a better word for it? Of course, she wasn't like *most* grandmothers, was she? When she was mad, boy howdy, she was mad! But when she was happy, wow. She was a force of nature."

Mom reached for a tissue and blew her nose. "I wish we'd made it back up here more often to see her. I wish we'd lived closer. But oh, she loved you, Annie, and how you made her laugh. Nobody laughed like Mom. I'll always remember her that way, laughing. Won't you?"

And then the strangest thing happened. Suddenly I did. A picture was forming in my mind of a tall thin woman with a head of gray curls, laughing. Her dark eyes snapping, her head tossed back. And somewhere in that face was Molly, *my* Molly, laughing too. Molly, her arms in a trash can. Molly on a fire escape. Molly, her quick fingers braiding my hair.

Then Molly was fading away, into the fog, and the gray-haired lady was back, and I was remembering moments. A day at the beach. A club sandwich. A bedtime story. A fight over a green jacket. A morning of baking Christmas cookies. And beneath all of that—a word, a single word, surfacing in my mind, bubbling up. "Yeah," I said. "Yeah, she could laugh. Gosh, could she ever. Nobody laughed like . . . *Gran.*"

Then that was all there had ever been.

POSTMORTEM

The next morning Mom looked rumpled, with big bags under her eyes. Still, there was a ton to do, so she didn't even bother to shower. She just chugged three cups of coffee in the café while I ate my waffles. Then we went back upstairs so she could put on some lipstick and call Aunt Ginny and Aunt Maggie to break the news.

While I made the bed and did the dishes in the sink, Mom sorted the bills that had piled up on the desk while Gran was so sick. She looked stressed. "I'll need to call a lawyer about this stuff. I don't know what kind of magic Mom's used to keep this place running all these years. It's so freaking complicated."

Gran didn't want a funeral. She'd asked to be cremated

and cast into the harbor, but we still had to visit the mortuary so Mom could sign a bunch of papers. I hated that place, with its slick leather furniture, and the shelves full of fancy death jars. Everything glossy and cold.

Back at the hotel, we rummaged in Gran's jewelry box and closet. Mom sorted out the plastic pop beads from the pearls, while I tried on Gran's rainbow of ball gowns from the fifties. Then we pawed through the knickknacks on her dresser together, little boxes full of dried corsages, fortune cookie fortunes, lost buttons, and one tiny tarnished spoon. After a few hours, we made tea and ordered up a round of Sneakypies, our favorite Hotel Calvert specialty, full of jam and cream to sustain us.

We packed a big trunk with the things we didn't trust the movers with—Gran's journals, the dolls she'd been collecting since she was a kid, her letters and pictures. There were *so* many pictures.

Gran's photo albums were full of hazy memories, moments I could barely recall—Gran holding me up to an elephant at the zoo. Gran reading to me from her old copy of *The Secret Garden*. Gran watching me smash a cake on my first birthday. There were also people I didn't recognize in the pictures, people she'd worked with at the Woolworth's lunch counter, girls from her college, as well as folks she'd met on the jillion trips she'd taken over the years. A week in Paris, an African safari. Gran had made friends everywhere.

It got late. Mom crashed for a while on the couch, but I kept working. When she woke up, I was leafing through the very last scrapbook. It was blue, with gold letters on the front that read MY SCHOOL DAYS. Mom raised herself off the couch and stared at me with bleary eyes. "Got anything good there?"

"Oh, just Gran." I smiled. "I found this insane list she made. Pages of stuff she wanted to do someday—visit the pyramids, meet Fred Astaire, eat an entire lemon pie. What's funny is that a lot of it is stuff *I've* always wanted to do. But guess how many she checked off. . . ." I shuffled through the pages.

Mom laughed. "Knowing Gran, I'm guessing all of them. Even Fred Astaire."

"Yep," I said. "All except one. She never became a nurse. It's circled. I wonder why she wanted to do *that*?"

"No telling," said Mom. "Hey—you know what *I* want to do? Eat a cheeseburger at the Buttery. With a vanilla milk shake. Right now. How about you?"

I nodded. "Sure, yeah." But when I stood up, the scrapbook fell from my hands and hit the floor, where it split open along its spine. "Oh, Mom, I'm sorry," I said, reaching for the pieces.

"It's nothing we can't fix with tape," Mom said, sliding on her clogs. She finger-combed her hair. "Leave it. We have more important matters to address. I want mine with extra pickles."

"Okay," I said. But as I set the two halves of the scrapbook in the trunk, with all the news clippings and old dance cards, a single picture came loose and fluttered to the floor. When I reached to pick it up, I found myself staring down at a strip of photo-booth shots. Black-and-white images of two blurry girls. One was Gran, for sure. The other was a faded face I'd never seen before. Yet somehow, despite the scratched and stained photo, she looked familiar.

In the top shots, the girls were startled, unready. But in the last frame, Gran was hugging the other girl, with a huge smile, a fierce grin. *That* was Gran all over. Fierce. I stared at the picture.

"Hey, Mom!" I called. She was already at the door, waiting for me, her purse over one shoulder. "Mom, wait! Do you know who *this* is?" I held out the picture.

"Whatcha got?" Mom asked.

I pointed. "This girl with the braid. Is she a cousin? She looks like Gran, doesn't she?"

Mom peered down at the picture and chuckled. "You're right, there's a resemblance. But she's actually not related. I'm sure Gran mentioned Annie to you. She kept that picture taped to her vanity for years."

I shook my head. "I don't think so." Then I looked again. "Really? *Annie?*"

"Yep," said Mom. "I *know* Gran told you this story when you were little. You should listen better, kiddo. She was Gran's best friend, but Annie got sick or something and moved away. I'm not exactly sure about the details. Maybe she even died? If memory serves, her family stayed in the hotel one summer."

I shook my head. "No, I don't remember anyone telling me this."

Mom laughed. "Gran *insisted* we name you after her. She put her foot down about it, and you know how things went when Gran put her foot down."

I smiled. "Yeah."

"*That's* why your legal name is Annie, not Anne."

"Wow, I was named for some random kid you never even met?"

"Pretty much," Mom said. "Though of course, if she's still around, she's not a kid anymore. She'd be Gran's age now."

I stared at the picture a little longer, then slipped it into my pocket as Mom reached for the door. "Come on, kiddo," she said. "Time for supper. Past time."

So we left the apartment, made our way through the hallways, down the elevator, into the lobby, where we waved goodbye to Anderson the concierge and Hassle the cat, latest in a long line of Hotel Calvert tabbies. We stepped out beneath the trees and street lamps onto the familiar gray bricks.

There was a soft breeze, and the moon was out. The Washington Monument gleamed white above us. The hotel windows were all lit up and golden. It was a perfect night, except for one thing. There was an ache, just beneath my ribs.

"I'll miss this place," I said. "I'll miss it a lot."

"Of course you will," said Mom gently. She put an arm around me. "I'll miss it too. But you know, we can always come back."

"Yeah," I said. "Only it won't be the same."

Mom stared at me a minute, then slowly she shook her head. "No," she said. "I won't lie to you. *Nothing* will be the same. But after a little while it will get easier. We were lucky to have her as long as we did. Try to think about it that way."

I closed my eyes and felt the tears in them. I nodded.

"She loved you *so* much, Annie," said Mom. "More than just about anyone."

I nodded again, as a horn honked in the distance. "I loved her too."

"She knew that," said Mom. Then she grinned and shouted out, "Jeez, enough with all the feelings, already. I need a milk shake to go with my sadness. Let's move!" She started walking quickly toward Charles Street.

But I didn't follow her right away. I stood there on the sidewalk, alone, for one more second. I took a deep breath, and I smiled. Because suddenly the air smelled like cinnamon.

It was nice.

AUTHOR'S NOTE

I've always loved old things. Antiques stores full of junk jewelry. Faded black-and-white photographs. Dusty dolls with china heads. Remnants of the past.

But if you'd asked me when I was a kid whether I liked History, I'd have shouted, "No way!" I thought History (with a capital *H*) meant memorizing a timeline of major world events. The Battle of the Bulge. The Magna Carta. President Roosevelt's birthday. *Boring.*

So when I started to write this book, I didn't think of *Seven Stories Up* as History at all. I only wanted to set a magical adventure in the awesome old hotel where my grandmother grew up. This book was personal, rooted in my own weird family saga. It was going to be fiction. It was going to be magical.

But you know what? This book took me three years to write precisely because it *is* History. My family is History as much as the Battle of the Bulge is. *Your* family is History too. Along with every black-and-white photograph or china-doll head you've got.

Because when you tiptoe into the past, it's impossible to separate personal details from major world events.

History is the fabric of everything that's ever happened, all woven together. My family and your family and President Roosevelt's family are interconnected. From the Magna Carta to the roller skates you got for your seventh birthday. All of this is History.

Seven Stories Up took three years to write because when I realized I was writing History, I had to check all my facts. What was the price of a candy bar?[1] What did underpants look like?[2] Did Ferris wheels exist?[3] How about kitty litter?[4] These are the things I spent three years looking up. Seriously, I researched the history of kitty litter.

The thing is that the whole time I was researching the little details, I was also researching those major world events I'd found so boring as a kid. Because you can't separate the Depression from the price of a candy bar in 1937. They're one and the same. You can't write a time-travel book where a kid arrives in 1937 and have her *not* notice segregation. Even if major world events are not

---

1 Surprisingly little! The answer is on page 72.

2 Kind of ugly, really. See page 38 for the answer, or better yet, find a book with a picture.

3 Yes, totally, and a description can be found on page 155.

4 Nope, but that didn't stop people from setting up cat boxes. Check out page 164 to see what they used instead.

what the story is about, they're inextricably linked to the city streets your main character is walking along.

And the more you focus on those streets, those personal details, the less boring History becomes. The more true you make your story, the more magical it will be.

So, just in case you're interested, here's some extra History, with a capital H. If you dig a little deeper and start hunting details yourself, you might be shocked at how fascinating it all is.

* * *

CHILD LABOR

Life for a ten-year-old in 1937 was in many ways the same as life today, but in other ways it was totally different. Most kids attended some kind of school, but plenty didn't. Instead they worked long days in textile mills and coal mines. Can you imagine standing for twelve hours straight, at a big dangerous machine in a sweaty smoky room, hungry and thirsty the whole time?

It wasn't until 1938 that a law was passed that regulated child labor in the United States, the Fair Labor Standards Act. After 1938, kids under sixteen were no longer allowed to work during school hours, and kids under eighteen were not allowed to work at especially dangerous jobs. But in 1937, when this book is set, there were no such federal laws. Molly was from a wealthy family, but Annika and Olivia might well have ended up doing such work.

THE GREAT DEPRESSION

Molly is in a strange position, as a lonely wealthy girl, isolated from the world outside her window. She is not aware of the massive poverty of her era, even though it is surely affecting almost everyone who passes through the Hotel Calvert.

The Depression that began with the "Black Thursday" stock market crash in 1929—when some people jumped out of windows because they were so devastated by sudden financial ruin—was slowly improving in 1937, but there were still many Americans out of work. Breadlines and soup kitchens helped to ease the suffering of many, but lines were long and hunger was rampant. Suicide rates rose, and violence increased. At the peak of the Depression, nearly 25 percent of American workers were unemployed. Many families lived in makeshift homeless encampments called Hoovervilles, and others left home in search of work. Molly hasn't spent much time with people like this, but Nora probably has!

THE HOLOCAUST

Even though this story isn't about the holocaust, I couldn't write about 1937 without hinting at what was happening in Hitler's Germany. While most Americans had no clue about the concentration camps, for European Jews, deportations and harsh restrictions were an increasingly stark reality.

Bayla's story—that of a child sent away to America for her own safety—was not uncommon. The sad thing to remember is that Bayla, though she is an orphan, is fortunate. The rest of her family, trapped in Poland, will likely have their homes confiscated and be sent to perish in the gas chambers or labor camps.

MEDICINE

When you get sick, you probably see a doctor, who gives you medicine to help you feel better. That makes it hard to imagine how the world was before so many of these medicines were invented.

Today, Molly's asthma would be treated with inhalers and pills, but believe it or not, in 1937, a lot of people felt that asthma was an imagined illness. A child's wheeze was thought to be an emotional cry for her mother. In the book, Molly is being treated by a family doctor, as a follow-up to her bout of pneumonia, but in truth, there was little that could be done for her long-term. She'd spend her life as an invalid.

Additionally, in 1937, penicillin had not yet been widely introduced, and people regularly died of minor illnesses and infections. Vaccines for deadly illnesses like polio were being discovered, but they weren't yet available to the public. In general, medicine was a very different experience. People who went to the hospital often didn't come home, and many people feared doctors as a result.

RADIO

In Baltimore in 1937, Molly would not have had access to a television. TVs were just being developed at that time (largely in the New York area). Radio shows were still the main form of entertainment in the home. Especially during the Depression, when people couldn't afford to go out, the radio was at the center of many homes. A radio back then looked more like a piece of furniture, built of wood, with heavy tubes inside it. It cost around fifty dollars, which was more than a week's pay for the average American.

Many early TV shows began in radio, from soap operas like *Guiding Light*, (which only went off the air as a TV show in 2009) to family programs like *Little Orphan*

Annie. The radio was also one way for President Franklin Roosevelt to communicate with the country, through his fireside chats. Families would gather around the radio for news, music, and laughter.

SEGREGATION

This is hard to imagine today, but until the landmark *Brown v. Board of Education* case in 1954, schools were typically segregated. In Baltimore until 1948, neighborhoods could be legally segregated to exclude Jewish and black families. Shops and restaurants were segregated, and so were theaters and trolleys.

It is only in places of work—the market and the docks—that Annie sees everyone working together and realizes what a bubble she's been experiencing at the hotel, and in the neighborhood surrounding it. In fact, African American Baltimore was a vibrant community, with beautiful theaters, restaurants, and hotels of its own, as well as black colleges and churches. In the 1930s, it was home to important Americans like the singer Billie Holiday and Thurgood Marshall, who argued and won the historic *Brown v. Board of Education* case mentioned above. In 1937, however, because of segregation, Molly and Annie would never have crossed paths with either of them.

* * *

If you want to learn more about any of these topics, I highly encourage you to do a little digging on your own. In some ways, History is the wildest, most improbable story you'll ever read. Truth is, as they say, "stranger than fiction." So do yourself a favor and hunt for the details, starting with things you know you enjoy.

If you love basketball, begin there. If you like ninjas, research those. If you're addicted to cartoons, try reading up on some old ones. Or begin with your own family, the same way I did with *Seven Stories Up*. Pull out an old family photo album, and ask questions about the people you find there.

What you'll discover is that with any topic, the smallest bits of History will interweave with the greatest events of the age. Because everything is History. Including you! On any given day, just walking down the street or reading a book, *you're* becoming part of History.

Pretty cool, right?

ACKNOWLEDGMENTS

Anne Conway Hamill Dietz

This book belongs to my grandmother, Anne Conway Hamill Dietz.

When I was a kid, she seemed like a magical creature to me, eccentric and full of wonder. Among other things, she was a children's librarian who scoured the bookstores of Southern California to send me signed first editions.

But as we both grew older, it became clear to me that my grandmother was not a happy person. In the final years of her life, she isolated herself. This was difficult for everyone in the family. I can't begin to explain. . . .

The last time I flew to California to see her, her heart was failing. She was in physical pain, but beyond that, she was revisiting hard memories of a childhood spent (amazingly) in a grand hotel. "Like Eloise," she'd told me when I was little. Only *this* didn't sound like Eloise.

I didn't know how to help her, so I just listened. The

last hour I spent with her, in the hospital, she kept going back to one particular summer, a lonely season spent in quarantine because she had rheumatic fever.

After she died, I returned over and over to that image—of a kid, locked away at the top of a hotel, in unrelenting solitude. Some part of me wished that I could open the door to her room, that I could lead her out.

And so (as often happens in the magical world of children's books) my wish became a seed, and the story of Molly and Annie took root, blossomed.

This book is fiction. Molly is *not* my grandmother. But I do hope that wherever she is, my grandmother knows I've spent the last three years thinking about her daily, staring at her picture, and trying to make something happy from her saddest memory—a memorial to a singular woman, who lived through more than one lonely summer.

"Magic is what people call it when the universe corrects itself," says Fortunata in the pages of this book. We do what we can to help it along.

* * *

Of course, this book does not belong *only* to my grandmother. It went through many drafts, and many early readers. Massive thanks to: Emma Snyder, Rachel Zucker,

Marc Fitten, Kate Milford, Sally Burke, Lisa Brown, Natalie Blitt, Gwenda Bond and Beth Revis, along with the other members of the Bat Cave Writers' Retreat, Jennifer Laughran, Cynthia Von Buhler, Rebekah Goode-Peoples, Elizabeth Lenhard, and especially Paula Willey, who not only read this in its roughest state, but also helped me look up all sorts of weird 1937 Baltimore facts, librarian-goddess that she is!

As always, I'm grateful for the constant support of my dear friend Tina Wexler, who also happens to be my literary agent (lucky for me). I'd have thrown the second draft from a bridge if she hadn't been there to talk me down.

And *Seven Stories Up* could not possibly exist without the very sharp eyes and endless patience of my editor, Mallory Loehr. She's what people imagine when they picture a true editor: committed, insightful, smarter than me.

I also want to thank everyone at Random House who contributed to this book—Alison Kolani, Paul Samuelson, Tracy Lerner, Tim Jessell, Nicole de las Heras, Jenna Lettice, and Lisa Nadel. I'm lucky to have such a great team.

I suppose I should also acknowledge my fantastic

parents, who never locked me up in a hotel room. Not even in high school, when I probably deserved it.

Last but not least, I want to thank my family. My husband, Chris Poma, who (almost) never complains when I turn on the light in the middle of the night to scribble. And my hilarious, wild, beamish boys, Mose and Lewis. *We* are never alone.

LAUREL SNYDER

(age 11)

Laurel Snyder is the author of many books for kids, including *Bigger than a Bread Box*, *Penny Dreadful*, and *Any Which Wall*. Though she now resides quite happily in Atlanta, she will always be a little homesick for her native Baltimore.